NORTH

by

M.H. VESSEUR

NORTH

The Hitomi Files: One

A novel by

M.H. Vesseur

Vibes Publishing

Published by Vibes
www.mhvesseur.com
www.facebook.com/MHVesseur

Version 1.0
ISBN 978-94-91908-24-8 (paperback)
ISBN 978-94-91908-23-1 (Kindle epub with DRM)
ISBN 978-94-91908-22-4 (epub with DRM for Apple iBooks
and Kobo)

THE HITOMI FILES

North

Part I

"In the East, the sun rises full of hope.

In the West, it sets in confusion.

In the North, it is sometimes forgotten."

—From the diary of Hitomi Sakamoto

In the second half of the 20th century.

One

This world knows two kinds of secret laboratories. The first kind is stacked away in remote places, such as mountains or deserts or industrial zones. They have the advantage of being remote, but once you get there, they really draw your attention. But we'll get to that type of laboratory later.

The second kind is simply located in big cities, right under — or above — the nose of millions of people. That's the kind of laboratory where this story starts.

It was located in a very large city, in one of those buildings nobody looks at. Tourists looked at architectural marvels and residents looked at nothing because they were used to the view and in a hurry to get somewhere. It was a tall office building, made out of concrete and glass and marble, and it was neither ugly nor beautiful, it just stood there and it was of no interest to no one. There was a sign with hundreds of company names on the ground floor. There were no shops in the street and the people going in and out of the buildings used taxis and other cars. It was a business environment and that meant that everybody was being very practical about everything.

There were nice flowers on the ground floor though, in a huge vase on the marble floor near the reception, where two ladies tended to the visitors and where security people stopped by every now and then.

On the twenty-seventh floor we find our laboratory.

Let's suppose you got there by elevator. The sign next to the button with the number 27 said 'Everest Inc.', which was also the case next to the numbers 25, 26, 28 and 29.

When you got out, you saw a small hallway with only three doors: one to the lavatories, one to the emergency stairway and one with another sign that said 'Personnel only'.

You can't go through that door, so I'll tell you what it looked like in there and what happened.

What happened is not a pretty picture, I must warn you.

The petri dish stood safely in the middle of the laboratory table. It contained nothing special, only fluid in which swam single-celled organisms taken from the test animals.

The laboratory assistant, a young man in a white coat, rummaged around the table covered by electronic equipment. On face value, the lab assistant looked almost too young to have any experience whatsoever. He was handsome, his long red hair in a knot on top of his head. Even though he was obviously slim and athletic underneath his white laboratory coat, he moved around clumsily like a rookie; he felt like a rookie anyway. *This is not my day. Fortunately the profs are out for their coffee break. If they could see me now they'd scold me for delaying the proceedings.*

The proceedings were: make fast progress with the bacterial cultures. The company who owned the laboratory, Everest Inc., was a large pharmaceutical company in search of profitable medicines for the near future; the nearer the better. It takes time to find cures. And once they're found and brought to the markets around the world, other companies would follow soon. Patents were only profitable for a short period of time, thanks to international laws. Therefore Everest had to come up with new medicines regularly. It was a race against time; or rather a rat race against other companies. Losers went bankrupt. Employees of losers went unemployed.

The reality of it was actually harsh: if a young assistant didn't over-perform, he'd be fired right away. There were dozens of other assistants ready to take over his job.

A bacterial culture could produce results after twenty-four hours, but it could also take several days, and then you'd have to start over again. So the more cultures he could prepare for testing in a day, the better. There was a large list in the computer of tests that had been done and had yet to be done, and he was falling behind.

He had received an official warning early that morning.

"You have to meet the targets or we have to say goodbye," he had been told.

They're not that nice. They pretend they're nice, but they're not.

So now the young lab assistant was rushing it.

Which was funny, because there were two things forbidden in the laboratory:

not meeting targets,

and rushing to meet targets.

The young laboratory assistant was looking for a lamp. He had been working for hours and was tired. He'd been unable to find the right light for quite some time, but finally stumbled upon it. He turned it on but its battery was out of juice. He needed to plug it in before he could proceed, so he pushed a plug into the wall outlet and took the end of the charging cord to the lamp.

But the cord slipped from his fingers and fell into the petri dish and sent electrical sparks upwards. It produced a tiny symphony of ticking sounds. The fluid in the petri dish radiated a bright light for a moment and then the power from the outlet stopped. It had short-circuited.

Great. Now he had to go crawl on the floor again to find another outlet before he could commence and try to make up for lost time. The culture in the petri dish had to go back into the refrigerator before the high temperature in the laboratory could ruin it.

He didn't see the bright light in the petri dish fluid. Nor did he see the microscopic movement of fusion inside the fluid. By the time he came back up from the floor, the light was gone and the movement had subsided.

The assistant did notice a strange smell though; like the clean air after a thunderstorm, but with something added to it that reminded him of animals in a cage. It was too vague to pay attention to and so he didn't.

Half an hour later the contamination alarm went off. The two scientists in charge of the laboratory returned from their break, as fast as they could without spilling their coffee and looked through the glass window.

Their young assistant made gestures at them. He wanted out, no question about it.

"It seems we're on to something," said one of the scientists. He pressed a button and started to talk calmingly to the panicked young man on the other side of the glass.

The young assistant was bathing in white light. The floor, the walls, the ceiling, the tables, the refrigerators and the chairs and the equipment. The light reflected the hell out of the place. Only a few utilities in the entire space were not white, like the crawling cellular organisms on the computer monitors. Or the blue logo of the world's largest pharmaceutical company, Everest Inc., pictured on the white coats of the young assistant and his superiors, computer terminals, windows, the door and the notepads.

"You must relax," said professor Van Hagen into the microphone. "You are in good hands. Think of it this way: if there's a heaven, it must be as bright as this place."

Van Hagen was a tall man, clean shaven, his graying hair curling on top of a charming face, with dimples and blue eyes.

His physique too impressive to be diminished by the clumsy white laboratory coat he wore.

Compared to Van Hagen, his colleague looked like a clumsy scientist from a funny movie. His name was professor Carreidas. His eyes looked huge through his thick glasses. His belly protruded in the laboratory coat and his face was pockmarked, crowned by the remains of a decaying hairdo.

But they were equally gentle, friendly and intelligent, and with a joke every now and then they improved their mood. Especially in difficult moments like this.

Fortunately, the young assistant in the laboratory relaxed somewhat. His features were partly hidden by a surgical mask and his hands were wrapped in white plastic gloves.

Carreidas added to the general mood of relaxation during the crisis by saying into the microphone: "Here on earth you have had the advantage of good looks. But in heaven there's a romantic lighting, you know, candlelight and soft music, so I will look as good as you up there."

"You are confusing heaven and hell," said Van Hagen.

That would soon prove to be a profound statement.

"We are now taking samples of the air," said Carreidas in to the microphone.

"I don't like it one bit," said the young assistant.

"It's probably nothing," said Carreidas in his most soothing tone. Outwardly he tried to calm his assistant's nerves, but inwardly he was very concerned.

He switched off the microphone.

"You think he got too close to the animals?"

"It makes no difference. We must check the air as well as his blood. Only then will we know where we stand."

Van Hagen and Carreidas soon put on airtight suits and moved into the sealed laboratory, through the vacuum chamber. Their young assistant sat on the floor slumped against the wall. Red dots covered his face, as if a swarm of mosquitos had visited him moments earlier. Blood dripped from one side of his nose onto the surgical mask that hung around his throat. "I don't feel well," he whispered.

"In the snow, we can abandon all our colors, leave behind the person we came to be. We can forget compromise. In the snow, I am white, and I can color myself all over again. For me, it is a necessary state of mind in between the past and the immediate future."

—From the diary of Hitomi Sakamoto

Two

—*Eastern hemisphere*—

Kiyoshiro possessed more karate experience than the hundreds of pupils from all of his classes of the past decade combined. Even his most talented student would eventually be no more than his equal, and remain on that level indefinitely. Kiyoshiro — a rather tall man by Japanese standards, so thin that his skin accentuated his skeleton rather than hid it — had been accustomed to this for at least a decade and thought of this as a natural thing, so he was never surprised, never taken off guard, never nervous.

In the case of this new pupil, a twelve-year old girl who had just moved into town, that was a grave mistake.

The tiny courtyard of Kiyoshiro's school was surrounded by walls of bamboo. Man-sized bonsai trees threw shades on the round rocks. Ivy tried to take over but was always cut back in the spring. Yellow grass, treaded and worn, covered the ground. In front of one of the four surrounding bamboo walls

— the one with the door — was a hardwood terrace. Placed on it were chairs and a table and a whole series of small mats. From the wooden terrace it was only a small step down onto the grass square in the middle. Alongside the other bamboo walls were large rocks and some bonsai trees.

The grass in the middle formed a square, large enough for dozens of pupils to engage in training.

Ten pupils were on the hardwood terrace in the 'seiza', the kneeling position. They waited while the new girl stepped forward on Kiyoshiro's request, onto the large training mat.

For a twelve-year old, the girl was surprisingly mature. Before class, the other pupils would giggle and laugh and sometimes even scream or run around. But not this girl, this... *What's her name again?* Kiyoshiro wondered. *Oh yes, Hitomi Sakamoto. 'Hitomi' means something like 'pupil of the eye'.*

Kiyoshiro could see immediately that it was a name well chosen. From a face that betrayed nothing, two almond shaped eyes stared at him almost as if they had been designed for maximum charming effect. Of course, being a teacher meant that Kiyoshiro kept a healthy distance to his pupils; he was never affected by beauty because of his intense concentration on the task at hand. But there he was: facing that one exception. It wasn't so much that Hitomi's eyes distracted him in any way. He just noticed.

He also noticed that she possessed the perfect athletic body, slim, muscular, moving elegantly across the mat. Her skin was pale and her black hair tied in a ponytail that reached down and touched her buttocks.

Finally, he saw Hitomi's hands move as she walked, and it made him think of a geisha. A very small gesture, alongside her hips, almost too small to notice, but he noticed it nonetheless.

He smiled, faintly enough so to that no one would notice.

The girl bowed to a shrine and then to Kiyoshiro and said: "Onegaishimas."

Kiyoshiro had expected her to say this word, which meant "please teach me," but he had not expected the faint smile that the girl's lips produced at the same time. He even doubted it. Had he imagined the smile? Was he unfocused? If there had been a smile on her face, it had been unconvincingly faint — a mere suggestion. If it was for real, it could have been meant to throw him off his guard. It could also have been mere uncertainty on the part of the girl.

After the introductory ritual, Kiyoshiro tested her abilities. The girl had had lessons in the town where she had lived before, but Kiyoshiro didn't remember the details he was told and it didn't matter. He would simply start at a twelve year old's level and overpower her. Get a grip on her or floor her, as he would usually do with new pupils.

In the instant before Kiyoshiro made his move, however, the girl shifted and swirled. Kiyoshiro was flat on his back. The girl bowed over him and said in a soft voice: "Kiyoshiro-san."

He was too shocked to respond immediately. He got up and bowed. Hitomi bowed back.

"Hitomi-san. We can all learn from you, no doubt," he said.

Then he smiled, but it was a forced smile, only to take away any possible attention from his intense embarrassment.

He failed to see the insecurity in the young girl's eyes; for she was just as shocked by the outcome of her aggressive approach as her new teacher was.

Three

—Western hemisphere—

"No. No. No," said Van Hagen loudly. "It is a random occurrence. Much like creation itself. Merely a coincidence, but not something that can be repeated willfully."

They were on the highest floor of Everest Inc., in the fading light of the late afternoon. They were twenty-nine floors above street level. Outside were other buildings of approximately the same height, but also smaller and taller ones. This variety made for a confusing palette of sunlight. From one angle came a huge shadow, from another came a blinding white spot: the sun retreating behind some distant clouds, moving down towards an invisible horizon. The buildings were all glass and concrete, and because not a single sound got through the glass, the world outside remained strangely remote.

None of those present were remotely interested in the view from the windows anyway. Not the two men standing. Not the one man sitting behind the desk.

Van Hagen and Carreidas stood at the desk of a man they could barely see; not much more than his silhouette showed itself against the sundown. The room was poorly lit to begin with. The only lamp was behind them, next to the door through which they had entered.

The three men couldn't have been more different from each other. Van Hagen, the tall eminence, curling gray hair on top of his impressive physique. Carreidas, the smaller, clumsy-looking caricature of a scientist, complete with thick glasses, bending his upper torso slightly forward.

Sitting behind a huge, shining, hard-wood desk, sat the third person in the room, the kind of man that made people aware of his *body* before his personality. Wherever he went, his body came first. He occupied space.

His unmistakable fatness did not make him unattractive. His black hair was modelled with finesse. His black beard was trimmed and unobtrusive. He was dressed in a very elegant suit, with a silk blouse and a tie that could have been designed by Vincent van Gogh or Pablo Picasso. On the table lay a hat, a large Fedora model. Other than that, the table was empty. The man spoke crystal clear and very rapid, very becoming of a man who was in charge of one of the world's largest pharmaceutical companies.

"For everything I do I must have the approval of the board," said the fat man softly. "Your report is not a story I can explain to them. You are saying you have accidently created this virus. You don't know the history of its mutation.

You don't know why it happened. And now you want to preserve it and test it. At the same time you say you have lied to the authorities about your assistant's death."

There was a moment of silence.

"ARE YOU OUT OF YOUR FREAKING MINDS?"

"On the contrary, Sir," said Van Hagen. "This is a unique moment in history. The virus is obviously not spreading. It seems to attack at close range. It could be a weapon somewhere in the future. Not to be used, but to be demonstrated as a threat because of all the side effects, the risk of global nuclear warfare. Aren't we still in the Cold War? Aren't nuclear weapons losing their strength as a threat? This virus can be the perfect replacement because it can be used on a small scale to demonstrate our strength and scare the enemy into submission. We have to think about terrorism and the state of the world, and the position of our nation."

"I am not interested in that," said the fat man. "My board and my shareholders want my throat for not making enough profits, for not reaching the one hundred billion mark quick enough. The government hates my guts for making profits abroad and not paying taxes at home. The general public hates my guts because of my bonus. Insurance companies and hospitals and patients hate my guts because they think I let them pay too much for our medicines. The last thing I need is a biological weapon. It will be my undoing."

Carreidas finally sat down. "You are thinking short term, Sir."

Van Hagen took a deep breath, but the shadow in the chair

waved his arm. "Carry on, Carreidas."

"You will be retired in a few years. You will be out of the spotlight. By that time we won't even have begun to understand what this new organism is all about. If we unleash public scrutiny now, it will be taken out of our hands. If we keep it to ourselves, we may be able to turn it into something useful for this company in the future."

"Such as? A biological weapon? You want this company's name on that?"

"Not necessarily. If it can destroy a man in a matter of days, perhaps it can also destroy something else, like other viruses. We must look into this. Like chemotherapy: you destroy certain cells with extreme force. What if we can turn this thing around and find, say, penicillin 2.0?"

The fat man sighed. "You are a convincing young man, Mr. Carreidas. I've never heard anyone say penicillin 2.0 before in my life, but it sounds good." He reached across his desk and picked up a phone. "Can you come up for a moment?"

The fat man stood up and turned towards the window, facing the edge of the sun as it sank beneath the buildings. This powerful glow in the sky kept most buildings in a dark pool for the time being. It would take another fifteen to twenty minutes for the sunlight to fade further and for the city to reveal itself again as a sea of lights under the stars.

"I want you guys to test this virus first," said the fat man. "Be discreet about it. Burlow is coming up to take you to our field site in Africa where you can fool around with it a bit. Go for just a tiny test that leaves no traces. Fly there, do it and fly back. Seventy-two hours max. Get that?"

Virus; a very small organism, smaller than a bacteria, that can't reproduce itself and is kept alive only by a host. Scientists still disagree on whether a virus is a lifeform or not. It can't be killed by antibiotics; only the immune system can do this.

Vaccine; an agent that boosts the immune system of the body for the fight against a virus. It helps the immune system prepare itself.

Four

In the 1970s the world was still full of shadows. A very convenient time for operations that could not be exposed to the raw light of day. There were no omnipresent media. There were still large zones of the planet outside reasonable regulations and laws. There were countries where the general population lived in obscurity, unaware of the new, emerging ethics of human rights and civil law.

So it was not very difficult for Van Hagen and Carreidas to find a place where they could carry out the small test that their immediate boss had asked for. They let Burlow — the firm's secret security guy, working enterily off-payroll — make the necessary arrangements.

It did take them two weeks to make the proper preparations though. And when they arrived on a remote airstrip of grass and gravel of some forest in Africa, they had to travel another three days by car on the worst road they had ever been on.

The kind of road that doesn't deserve a name; and doesn't have one.

But it served its purpose and it led them inland. The car was comfortable, although not even a Boeing's absorbers would have been able to deal with the holes they had to endure for three days.

Eventually they arrived in a remote place, where old buildings stood unused. They were stone buildings, left behind by former colonists and missionaries, a small village of houses and walls built around a church.

The lush forest whirled around the buildings like a green sea, while a hot wind rattled the leaves of trees and bushes, forcing the remains of a tropical rain to trickle further down to the red earth.

Carreidas got out of the car, utterly exhausted. His thick glasses were moist and dirty and his large belly was confused by all this jostling around — he felt quite sick. He rubbed his three-day beard and looked at his older colleague, professor Van Hagen. Carreidas had been looking at him for a long time and decided he didn't like what he saw, through his smeary glasses: quite miraculously, Van Hagen had been able to keep up appearances. He was shaven, his graying hair was locked in its eternal curl on top of his head and his clothes showed no signs of wearing. The man stepped out of the car and stood in the sticky earth, entirely untouched.

Even the team of security people that escorted them here was taken aback by the journey, their black outfits wrinkled and stained with mud, their faces unshaven.

Fortunately, the fresh smell of the forest after the rain gave Carreidas new energy.

They followed Burlow off the road as he led the way in the opposite direction of old buildings onto a small path that for a moment seemed to lead them nowhere. After a couple of minutes it opened up to a small clearing in the African forest. On the other side stood a barrack, a building of rusty metal, with a corrugated roof and a few windows that were painted black. The building had clearly been there for a very long time; the foliage was growing across the roof on one side.

But it was still accessible. The front, where a large door without windows was situated, had been kept clear: fresh cuts were visible in the bushes. Trees had been cut. In front of the barrack, two men in military uniforms waited for the visitors. The difference between the two of them couldn't be greater: one was a soldier in a very simple combat outfit, wearing a machine gun and mirroring glasses, the other wore a military suit with officer's stripes covering his shoulder pads. They had little in common beyond the army clothes and large whiskers and a very white smile that contrasted starkly with their dark skins. The soldier with the gun was thin and muscular and slightly nervous. The officer was large and self-confident and would make a fine lookalike for dictator Idi Amin.

This can be any country in Africa, Carreidas thought.

He had been informed about the exact location, but in the course of the journey he had lost track and forgotten names.

By now, he realized it didn't matter one little bit.

An anonymous country, ruled by an anonymous army.

He tried to remember the origins of the little flags on the military uniforms but not a single thought came to him.

The officer shook hands with the Everest security boss and then approached Van Hagen and Carreidas. The officer's smile was so white it reminded Carreidas of his laboratory.

They all shook hands and exchanged names, and Carreidas thought: *At least we can speak English here.*

"I am honored to meet you, my dear professors," said the officer. "My country is proud to co-operate with Everest on the development of medicine for the people. We have taken measures. We have taken precautions. We have arranged the testing facility. I can assure you that is my mission to make sure you can do your testing to your full satisfaction. Please follow me inside where the preparations have been made and the, eh, how shall I put it," — the officer took off his glasses and winked — "*volunteers* are waiting."

While the party disappeared into the barrack, the sky darkened again, clouds gathered for some more rain. But the barrack's windows were darkened by shutters, and the voices coming from the inside disappeared under the blanket of rushing rain.

Five

The Palais Carinth looked as if its designer had fused two time periods together. Its lower parts were a former palace built in the nineteenth century, which allowed royalty to look at the world from behind its white, marble pillars. On top of its robust white stones a modern glass tower was built, rising up higher than most buildings in this continental mountain city. Its facade mirrored the outside world, shielding its visitors. The old royalty of the continent long gone, replaced by diplomats from opposing parts of the world, the separated zones of oil fields, collective farms and consumer markets.

In one of the luxurious rooms a meeting took place. It was but a small gathering.

Two men stood by the window. They looked like elderly statesmen, with their tailormade suits, their graying but impeccably stylized haircuts, their subdued manners.

They were hard to distinguish, but it could be done

nonetheless. One of them wore thick glasses, enlarging his eyes and, in a strange way, also his personality. The other man did not wear glasses.

"I trust Van Hagen and Carreidas completely, Locarn," said the man with the glasses. "I trust them because the fat man knows what he's doing. So I don't think there'll be any breach of silence. I don't think the media are going to pick this up."

"What about the local government, Lord Rand?" said Locarn. "What about those trigger happy military in the heart of darkness?"

"Just a local colonel, I believe. He's been given a large offshore bank account. So he's not going to turn it into an issue. Also, the whole thing has been contained by now; the disease is no longer spreading."

"I should hope not. How many of the volunteers have died after they got the injection?"

"Twenty-seven."

Locarn turned around and walked to the oval table. He poured coffee from a container into a white cup that wore the hotel logo. "I don't like any of it, no matter how big your confidence in Carreidas is. All this death! All this irreversible death. What if he can't contain it?"

"Then we better pray," said Lord Rand.

"Pray?"

"It doesn't matter, Locarn. The virus is contained now."

Lord Rand paced the room.

"You must look at the big picture. Governments today are dealing with peace demonstrations, hippies and the USSR.

They don't have time to bother us about a virus in a dark country. Besides, all of this is totally irrelevant. Once we get a vaccine for this virus, our profits will be going through the roof. We can then sell it to the army... What am I saying: we can sell it to ten armies."

"I don't care if you want to make a profit by selling stuff to a couple of dictators," said Locarn. "Just make one hundred percent sure Carreidas doesn't talk to any outsider."

"They'll think it came from rats or bats or monkeys," said Lord Rand. "Nothing in the virus points in the direction of Everest."

Rand was raised in a family of aristocrats who had been successful entrepreneurs for centuries. He knew the ins and outs of arms dealing, of selling nuclear stuff, of avoiding the scrutiny of governments without becoming an illegal business. He also knew the value of time.

"I don't want to imply that it is without danger," he continued, "because it is not. But we have time on our side. We stash the whole thing away somewhere out of view. We put Carreidas and Van Hagen in charge. I'll bet ten or twenty years from now they come up with an antidote and then we're ready to go. It's a normal investment. Thirty years max and we have the most powerful virus in our possession, including a vaccine. Signed, sealed delivered. Besides, there's more to that virus than our business. I've thought of this. It's the grand economy of the world that is at stake here. The world economy has always needed a crisis to get out of the slumps. Think about the second world war, that turned out to be the perfect catalyst for economic growth afterwards. The Vietnam War. The Cold War. All that has been good for business all over the place. If the economy ever crashes, one can release a virus. Everybody will forget about his bank account immediately and unite, get into the laboratories and into the hospitals to help."

"You have a morbid mind," said Locarn. He sighed. "I hope I'll be retired by the time anything needs to be done with this virus. I see your point but that doesn't mean I'm happy about it.'

He raised a finger from a fisted hand and pointed it at Lord Rand, shaking it. "Better put the buggers very far away and out of view."

"Somewhere close to the North Pole," said Lord Rand. "I can get us a facility that was an espionage center during the Second World War. It's very old, but it's also very remote and rather sturdy. It needs some fixing, but it can be done and it won't look suspicious. There will be no connection to Everest."

They shook hands.

"There will be nothing in the records and there will be no updates," said Locarn. "Double check."

Locard turned and walked towards the double doors. But he changed his mind about something and halted when he grabbed the doorknob, and turned.

"What?" snapped Lord Rand.

"We can never call it by its real name," said Locarn. "Just to be on the safe side."

"You mean Ebola?"

Locarn closed his eyes, a shade of pain hovering over his face.

He opened them, said "Make sure no one uses that word again until further notice," and walked out of the room.

Lord Rand smiled and turned his attention back to the view. Moments later, a young woman appeared. "Your car is waiting to take you to the airport, Lord Rand. Mr. Carreidas and Mr. Van Hagen will be joining you in Helsinki."

"How much time before the flight, Miss Rhondinova?"

"One hour."

"In that case we are going to my room first."

Lord Rand walked towards the woman. "I need some exercise before I'm strapped to a business class chair for hours again."

She gave him a faint smile and let him out of the room.

Six

Hitomi Sakamoto lived with her grandfather. He was her only relative. Or the only one she knew about other than her mother. Not that she had ever asked. Hitomi, at twelve years, was an observant child who never asked too many questions. She preferred the quiet way of listening carefully and being patient — which usually presented her with all the information she needed. And the information she didn't get, well, she felt she could do without that anyway.

She liked the idea of secrets existing, lingering in the air, perhaps forever, perhaps only for a while. The very idea of the Titanic laying on the bottom of the ocean, undiscovered, thrilled her to no end. She loved to read magazines with such stories. Lost ruins in the jungle. Ships full of treasures that had sunk and remained missing. The Bermuda triangle. The disappearance of the dinosaurs and the decline of the Mayan culture.

What little Hitomi knew about her mother and about the way she had died, people had told her.

No one had ever asked her: "Do you want to know about your mother?"

They had simply told her.

She now knew that the very idea of not wanting to know something, anything, was repulsive to people.

Even in the north of Japan, on Hokkaido. The culture that surrounded her praised patience and humility, but some of the people just couldn't keep their mouths shut.

Not her grandfather though. He taught her these things, patience and humility.

"When you are patient, time passes and brings you the things you need," her grandfather said to her often.

He was a wise man and she believed him. He had long white hair, which he wore in a ponytail, and he was quiet behind his beard — also white, like the mountain.

Only in that way — his white hairs — was he the opposite of Hitomi. In most other ways, they were the same. Slim. Muscular. Inquisitively. Suspicious. And resisting any kind of meddling from other people.

They lived at the foot of a mountain with a white top, close to a village, small but sufficient, and with a train station that was a gate to the world. He taught her how to hunt with the Japanese bow and arrows and cook food, and made sure she learned how to fight.

"In this country, a woman is not supposed to take care of herself, or be independent," he said. "That is a mistake. I will teach you how to take care of yourself in case something happens to me and you are left to yourself."

But he also taught her to not draw too much attention to her growing independence.

Hitomi Sakamoto was going to draw attention to herself sooner or later though.

Beating Hitomi Sakamoto soon became an obsession for Kiyoshiro. He was a proud man, for whom defeat by a pupil so young was close to unbearable. It was clear that the only escape from further embarrassment was to remove Hitomi from this class, but that truth hadn't dawned on him completely. He just had to try something else; that was his karma. So the next week he took his class on bow and arrow practice.

Kiyoshiro did some explaining, demonstrated his skills, shot some arrows into a wooden wall. There was a calming smell of trees and blossoms, the humming of birds and the faint trickle of water down a tiny stream nearby. They stood on the steep grassy knoll behind his sports school.

Kiyoshiro thought it was actually a pleasant lesson on a lovely day and was starting to forget his original goal. He hung up a board with a red dot and three circles around it and shot one arrow into the red dot from a distance.

Then he gave the Japanese bow to his new pupil, smiling behind his frozen face, anticipating her defeat.

Twelve-year old Hitomi Sakamoto took the bow and fired away.

Everyone looked on in breathless amazement as Kiyoshiro's arrow, firmly planted in the red dot on the board, was hit by Hitomi's arrow and forced from its position, and fell to the ground.

Kioshiro looked at Hitomi. There was not a hint of a smile on her face, but he found that hard to believe.

He looked around at the other pupils, but no one smiled. They all knew Kiyoshiro's sensitivities.

Then he bowed, a tiny bow towards Hitomi.

Just a lucky shot, Kiyoshiro tried to think, but he didn't succeed. He knew it wasn't just a lucky shot; he knew that young Hitomi was a talent in many ways. He also realized, for the first time since Hitomi had entered his classes, that he had to step up and be spiritual about all this. He had to rise to the occasion, above his small self, and see to it that this young girl would have the opportunity to expand her considerable talents.

However, he also had to put Hitomi in a separate class to keep himself from further embarrassment.

"You are very talented," said Hiyoshiro, when he sat with Hitomi in his teacher's office, after the other pupils had left.

"Thank you," said Hitomi.

"Now I know what your grandfather meant when he said that I should just wait and see. One has to see you in action to believe you."

They both drank their tea. Neither of them spoke until the tea bowls were entirely empty.

Then the teacher got up and bowed ever so slightly to Hitomi.

The girl also got out of her chair and returned the courtesy.

"You are going into a special future where others can't go," said Kiyoshiro. "I will help you to the best of my abilities. It is imperative that you don't draw too much attention to your talents because it will attract the wrong kind of people."

"What people?" asked Hitomi.

"People with power, be it good or bad. They will all want to use you for their own purposes. If you want to live a free life and decide for yourself, it is important that you first work on your talents for many years and stay out of view. Then, when you are ready, you can decide if you want to be in the limelight or remain in the realm of true humility. When one is young, one can be ambitious. Sometimes the appreciation of humility comes too late in life."

Kiyoshiro made a small gesture with his right hand, signaling that Hitomi was now allowed to leave the room.

The teacher sat down again and concentrated on his paperwork. No need to be distracted any further.

Part II

In the 21st century.

Seven

Hitomi Sakamoto's big city apartment was a long cry from her youth on Hokkaido. Her modern home was situated near the city's central park, overlooking the trees and the grasses, and the noisy streets and skyscrapers beyond. It wasn't large; no one with an average income could afford a large apartment in the city. But for a woman alone it was large enough — and most importantly, she had a small gym packed into a tiny room. All her training equipment at the ready at all times.

Hitomi preferred visiting the gym, but there were times when going there was inconvenient. Sometimes the rush hour would take her too much time. Often she just came off work too late to go to the gym. Sometimes she didn't need her personal trainer.

And there was another reason for withdrawing into her own private gym: the availability of an authentic, Japanese interior and utilities such as a bow and arrows. The room was not wide enough to allow serious long range practice, but she fired arrows into a board regularly nonetheless.

"Keep practicing every day," her grandfather had once said, long before she left for one of the big cities in the world, "for the skills you learn today will come in handy often."

She still believed there was a truth in that — even if it still remained to be proven.

This morning Hitomi was in no mood to go to the gym, for reasons unknown even to her. She had a feeling there was something keeping her at home until it was time to go to work. Her grandfather had taught her to listen to feelings, however inexplicable.

"They're there for a reason, even if that reason is shrouded by fog," he had said a long time ago.

Perhaps it is just as well, thought Hitomi. *Perhaps there is a visitor coming over or perhaps it is just nothing, like it usually is.*

There was no time to mull over it anyway. Work waited. She had to be in the business talk radio studio in a couple of hours and attend the editorial board meeting. As the radio show's producer she played a pivotal role to the success of the broadcast. That, and being the most important assistant to business talk radio show host Carl Pappas, her boss.

By the time Hitomi was done with her training schedule — a series of sit-ups, hanging down from a bar attached to the ceiling, slamming into a boxing ball for a while, and so forth — a voice came from the hall.

"Hitomi, it's me. Are you in?"

"Tired?" said Hitomi softly. "What have *you* got to be tired about?"

Her gym outfit showed the fruits of labor: wet spots in various places. A towel hung around her shoulders like a swollen noose.

As soon as Hitomi took out the band, her long black hair started to grab her face from all sides.

The young man standing in her living room looked very unhappy. This unhappy look didn't agree with the rest of him: he was all groomed and dressed for success. His suit was a dark gray, his hair was short and neat. His shoes were pointing to the latest fashion. But his face gave off the uncertainty of a young man worried about a woman's reaction.

The two of them raised eyebrows whenever they went somewhere together, that's how it was. Times don't change that much for couples from different origins. He was a tall office worker in his late twenties, slim but not athletic, and in spite of his youth and his good looks also a little boring once you got to know him. This type of young man had flooded the city in recent years, outnumbering the women.

She, on the other hand, was a petite Japanese woman in her forties, with long black hair and beautiful, almond shaped eyes that shone with energy. She had the body of a professional gym visitor, with a six-pack protruding through her clothes. Her hands moved like a Geisha's: gentle and with a purpose.

"Tired of having to listen to your opinion about everything, in general," he said.

Hitomi stood still and her mouth opened up, not much, just enough for air to slip through. She looked at him without speaking, moving the towel from left to right and back around her neck.

All her life, Hitomi had been consciously escaping the stereotype of the soft-spoken Japanese woman. Where she had grown up, women had power alright, but were never outspoken. As a result, Hitomi had developed a stubborn reluctance to keep her mouth shut about any topic. Not that she raised her voice; she felt no need to do that. Women who raised their voices all too easily became serpents in her eyes. It was important to remain completely feminine while speaking one's mind.

In doing so, she had become incessantly outspoken to some men, as if she was unable to look objectively at herself. This character trait, as it had developed, was on the other hand very useful in her job of supervising the world's most important business radio host. She was respected and feared because of this.

But outside of her work, this was a different matter altogether.

"You see? I say 'tired' and you attack that word immediately."

The mouth opened up further. This time, words did come out: "I didn't say anything!"

"But you were going to."

"Yes. That's fair. But... aren't you a modern man who likes his women outspoken?"

"Outspoken — yes. Aggressive — no."

"Who's aggressive? You've never protested for six months and all of a sudden you found some ammunition to blow me away?"

"Listen, Hitomi, it just wears me out. This is exactly what I mean. I have not kept my mouth shut for six months because, well, I like you, I like your outspokenness. But it's just... it's never ending. It all adds up and I get tired of it. Everything I say or do is scrutinized to the bone. I need a break."

He bent forward and kissed her on the cheek before she could reply or move away, and then he rushed out of the apartment.

I don't need this, Hitomi thought.

Her eye drifted towards the family portraits on the shelf next to the flat screen. Her mother stared back.

If I look at my mother, my mother looks back.

But her mother didn't just look back; she looked back across time. In the photograph, taken shortly before her death, she looked younger than Hitomi looked now. She was standing in a Japanese garden. Stones and leaves were capped by snow. A sad tree hung its branches downwards, but the woman looked happy.

Hitomi Sakamoto's mother was trapped in happiness in the maze of time, and stayed that way forever.

In a strange way this was always a comforting thought to Hitomi. By now, she had grown accustomed to the idea that one never gets over a tragedy, but sort of learns to live with it.

Like a scar: it'll always remind you of what happened, but it no longer hurts.

What the photograph didn't show, was also painfully present. The little brother. There were no photographs; Hitomi had to try and remember him without any visual aids. Those were the days in her home country, the North of Japan, when photographs were an anomaly — at least in her family. The picture of her mother was virtually the only one and it carried the heavy burden of having to tell multiple stories all on its own. From its faded surface a sadness emanated, only visible for Hitomi herself. Anyone else would only notice the cheerfulness on her mother's face and her subtle posture, the suggestion of a Geisha-like gesture. Anyone else would fail to notice the absence of the little brother in the yellow stains behind the glass.

And frankly, so did Hitomi Sakamoto most of the time. Because she had, by nature, a grip on her life and her feelings. Unless she was shaken and stirred like a James Bond Martini. And that's what had just happened. That stupid boy, whom she had taken as a chaperone for a couple of months, nothing special, just a guy to date and go to the movies with and chat — because that's what a single woman in the city did when she wanted to go out and not be bothered. That stupid boy, whom she had grown to like more and more, to a point where she began to like him maybe a little bit too much for her taste. She wasn't looking for a steady relationship while all her energy and focus went into her job as the executive producer of the business talk radio show The Boardroom — a monster of a show that was broadcasted worldwide to an astonishing audience of ten million business people. On the other hand, she was clever enough to allow something to grow, because she knew that's how life deals with your love life: you can't plan it.

And exactly at that moment, when something within her opened up, that stupid boy walked away. She preferred to ignore his goodbye altogether and remain as cold as ice, but it had already happened: the blow of him walking out had weakened her and now she was being touched by the image of her mother. It struck Hitomi once again how happy her mother's face was; because the story that was to destroy her, hadn't happened when the picture was taken.

Because how could that mother's face, glowing with happiness, know about the cold Hokkaido winter that was about to come, or how part of what she knew would melt away with the snow.

There are laws and one of them dictates the order of the seasons; fall and winter after the summer. Not the other way around. Time ends in winter.

So in the middle of this day, right after exercising in her own impromptu gym room, Hitomi imagined her little brother – not from what she had once seen, but from rumours and telltales.

In her imagination, her little brother walked under a ceiling of icicles. From an overhanging cliff, as a result of a leakage from the house on top of that cliff, a forest of ice picks had hung down, drawing the boy's interest.

One icicle had come down. It had been an odd coincidence

in a universe without meaning, and afterwards the mother had withered away in a darkness of her own.

She was dead on the first day of the following spring, leaving only little Hitomi in the care of her grandfather.

All this, the picture told Hitomi, while the image of the mother remained forever unaware of the fate that awaited her.

Hitomi reached out to the photograph and put it face down on the cupboard.

A cell phone buzzed.

Hitomi glanced at the screen, puzzled for a moment. Then she decided to answer the call.

"Sakamoto."

"Hitomi, it's Carl. Are we on for this afternoon's meeting? I think we should skip all topics and talk mainly about our radio format for next year. I need you to focus on that, give it all you got. Just shoot away, got it? Let's not be gentle. Let's give it hell. I'm counting on you."

What is it with men, she thought. *They don't really need a strong woman. Yes, they need it for business, and they need it to get turned on — but privately they need subservient women.*

"Sure, Carl, I'll be there and I'll be sharp as a knife," she said in her usual withdrawn way, sort of flat, matter-of-factly.

She switched off the cell phone, leaving her boss, the business radio talk show host Carl Pappas, puzzled, somewhere in cyberspace.

While Hitomi looked from her apartment into the city below, a bright wall of concrete and glass in the afternoon sun, she rubbed her neck with the towel.

But she didn't like the idea of a probable breakup with her boyfriend. The guy was never going to be the prince for her, but she had enjoyed it nevertheless.

No, it was this recurring issue that bothered her. This particular complaint; she'd heard it before. She'd been called a big mouth many times, for most of her life.

Behind her back, mostly — but still a heavy accusation for someone who talks with a soft voice.

It was not something she'd like to grow old with.

So, right there and then, she decided she needed a vacation away from the city, away from as many people as possible, right in the middle of nature, and take a deep breath and prepare for the next phase in her life; the after-the-last-boyfriend kind of life.

There was no way she was going to develop a clear thought about this while she worked. Hitomi's job ran on for seven days a week, the few off-hours usually spent working out or doing some unavoidable shopping.

Oh well, she had a whole hour with her boss that morning to convince him she needed the time off without her really telling him the true reason. That should work.

Eight

Most guests of the Palais Carinth found their way into the hotel bar only after their business had been concluded. It wasn't until five in the afternoon that they returned from their conference rooms in the eastern wing of the hotel or from other venues in the luxurious mountain city.

That meant that around three in the afternoon the place was usually empty. Therefore Lord Rand and Locarn had decided to have their annual chat about the Ebola antidote proceedings in the bar. Who was going to eavesdrop on them at this forsaken hour?

"I'll never get used to this way of dealing with things, even after all these years," Locarn complained. "All this money that flows into the project and I haven't even the slightest notion of what's going on out there."

"You seem to forget," said Lord Rand, "that as long as you don't hear anything, everything's fine."

"And you seem to forget that as long as I don't hear anything, there's one hundred percent lack of progress."

Lord Rand smiled. "Quite right my friend. To be completely honest, I was ready to propose calling the whole thing off today. But by some miracle there has been a breakthrough a couple of months ago."

Locarn raised his eyebrows.

The bartender arrived and offered each of them a glass of champagne.

Locarn raised it with a grin. "You have a flair for the dramatic, Lord Rand," he said when the bartender was gone again. "Hit me."

"We have an Ebola vaccine, Locarn," said Lord Rand.

They both got up from the Chesterfields and touched glasses.

"Within the foreseeable future you can start your own business, if you like, from the dividends of this medicine, Locarn."

"And what will you do?"

"I might retire," said Lord Rand. "I'm getting too old for the suspense."

They sat back down again.

"However, there are issues," said Lord Rand.

Locarn sighed. Then he turned, as a group of business people walked in, younger men and women coming off some seminar. They were talking loudly and were exhilarated, but they seated themselves at the bar, way beyond earshot.

"I don't doubt it. Hit me again."

"First of all, the only way Everest can ever make money on this ridiculously expensive medicine is to have a new Ebola outbreak."

"That can be arranged."

"Don't think of it as easy money, Locarn. If ever a connection between Ebola and Everest, or you and I, is made... You can't do anything with it until you are absolutely sure there is no connection between the origins of the virus and us. The whole medicine is worthless if that story comes out."

"I can wait," said Locarn. "There's no rush. Van Hagen retired last year. He's suffering from dementia in some old folks home. There's only Carreidas now and his assistant. Plus some security people who are unaware of the details."

"Make preparations for the transfer of the vaccine to an official Everest lab," said Lord Rand. "It's time to have someone accidently discover the vaccine. Carreidas and his assistant they must stay out of the picture. Put them away with a large bank account or else."

"What's the next issue?"

"Our main competitor has been sticking their nose into our affairs," said Lord Rand. "I don't think they've discovered anything, but they are prying. There has been espionage. There have been attempts to locate Carreidas."

"I'll put someone on it," said Locarn. "We are not going to give anything away without a fight. Are you sure Carreidas' location is absolutely safe?"

"Of course not. It's in the arctic, but it can still be reached. I mean, it's summer now, so the area is accessible. Sometimes there are tourists, there are a few outdoor cabins and there is the occasional hunter. I believe it is time to severe the connections. Move the production process to one of our normal laboratories. Fake a sudden breakthrough. And most of all: get rid of whoever is searching for Carreidas. I have received word that this guy is already quite close."

They finished their drinks.

"I can't move the production of the medicine to another location just like that," said Locarn. "It is going to take some time. No more than six months though. Anyway, it seems our patience is paying off."

While he talked, he noticed that Lord Rand's focus shifted to the young business people at the bar. A woman made a sudden movement, suggesting her craving for a hot dance, shaking her hips while raising a glass to a young man.

"Life is too short to be patient," said Lord Rand.

Dream on, thought Locarn, *you old fool. As soon as you are retired I am going to release Ebola and get filthy rich.*

Nine

The man in the dining car of the train wore a fine costume. Anyone could see that, though there weren't too many passengers around to do so. It gave him a distinguished look. His pitch-black hair was greased and combed back. Combined with a strong jaw, piercing blue eyes and a classic straight nose, it gave him the looks of a glossy magazine model — he was probably in his mid-thirties, athletic and with healthy skin. He was observing everything within view, but he kept it low-key; it was not an act of nervousness, but of perfectionism.

The low amount of passengers around him made sense: the train traveled through a remote mountain range in a country that can easily remain nameless because of its overall remoteness.

The man looked out the window for a moment. He noticed they were high up in the mountains and that the train was coughing up a black, unhealthy cloud.

The long body of carriages moved through the mountains

like a stubborn traveler, determined to reach his destination without detours and delays. It moved slowly up the slopes and then down again. It climbed and descended carefully, sometimes hiding in an endless tunnel, deep inside a mountain, for the longest time. Sometimes it rode a ridge and shone in the sun.

But most of the time it traveled in the shades of the mountains or the trees, rushing through the snow, coughing up pads of gray cotton.

In the late afternoon, the dining car was almost empty. In the rear, a couple chatted and ate at one of the tables. One man sat alone in the center. He paid no attention to the couple in the back. He drank red wine and read a book.

The waiter brought the man a plate with some hors d'oeuvres and a new glass of wine. The waiter looked at the book the man was reading and seemed to recognize the author's name, a famous poet.

How wonderful, the waiter thought, *to be alone on a trip through the mountains, and have the time and the peace of mind to read poetry.*

He smiled, but said nothing to the passenger, and let him be.

The passenger however did notice the waiter's smile. Even while he read, he noticed everything. At regular intervals, he took out an old watch that was chained to the inside of his jacket, and inspected the time. Then he read on.

By the time the poetry reader had finished his hors d'oeuvres, the waiter returned and put an envelope next to his plate.

"Please do excuse the interruption, Sir," he said. "But I have been requested to deliver this to you after finishing hors d'oeuvres."

The passenger nodded. "Thank you. I will take the main course in fifteen minutes, if that's all right for you."

"As you wish, Sir," said the waiter. He walked away.

The poetry reader took the knife from his plate and opened the envelope. He took out a letter and unfolded it. An uneven hand had written:

Meet me in wagon 4447, cabin 12.

Immediately, the passenger put the letter and the envelope in his jacket, got up and left the dining car.

The walk to train unit 4447 was quiet. The passenger met no one on the way over there. He had to walk four wagons and pass three icy corridors in between.

But there was no answer when he knocked quietly on cabin 12. He tried the door and found it unlocked.

He pushed the door open, moved into the dark cabin quickly and closed the door behind him.

Through the darkness he saw that the compartment window was open. A cold wind gushed in and made the curtains dance like circus horses. The chill affected him immediately. The cold light from the night sky reflected in the snow on the trees and the hills.

Then the lights came on and a voice behind him said: "Go on and close that window before we catch ourselves a death of cold, won't you, champ?"

The passenger turned around slowly and faced a man in an average business outfit; he looked like a worn out sales traveler, a family man on the road. His outdated mustache made him look tired, his pockmarked face pale and unhealthy in the unfriendly light of the luminescent tube. The gun he pointed was also very visible.

"Rogus Magnus, I might have known," the passenger said.

"Bruce Chapman, I might have known," the man with the gun replied. "Any other clichés you want to share with me?"

"Well, yes" said Chapman, "you could tell me if you've seen the passenger in this compartment. That cliché enough for you?"

"Very predictable indeed, Chapman. Listen, I have a message for you from my bosses: your company should back off. You hear me? Back off's the word."

He stepped closer to Chapman and pointed his gun towards the window for an instant. "And as for your passenger: he had to get off this train urgently."

That instant, when Rogus Magnus pointed his gun, was enough for Chapman to grab the weapon with one hand and work his arm around Magnus' neck. Magnus bent over and wriggled as much as he could, but he was no match for Chapman's muscle power.

"If we all find what we're looking for, asshole," hissed Chapman into Magnus' ear, "we'll just end up in another fight, because no one is going to allow someone else the prize. So I think one of us should call it a day and give the other some room."

"Over my dead body, Chapman," said Magnus with a hoarse voice, hardly able to breath. "Maybe I got some information from the passenger of this cabin that you would like to have, but only after you let me go."

"Good deal," said Chapman.

Then he turned around and ran towards the window with incredible force, Magnus still in the iron hold of his arm.

But Magnus stuck out a leg and they both tripped, face down to the floor. The gun fell away and the two men engaged in a wrestle match.

"Don't be stupid, Chapman," panted Magnus, "you need the information, you need my help. Boy, you're so dumb..."

He stretched out his hand across the floor towards the gun.

"And you have no heart," said Chapman as he worked himself up from the floor taking Magnus up with him, and kicking the gun further from them. "You throw a perfectly innocent informer of mine off this train and now he's lost in these mountains."

Then he lifted Magnus and pushed him up the windowsill.

"Be a good boy and show him the way back," he hissed into Magnus' ears and shoved him right out of the train.

The howling of the wind and the hammering of the train's wheels covered up any sound Rogus might have made during his journey to the ground next to the track.

Chapman closed the window and inspected the cabin. If there had ever been a passenger, he had certainly left not a single trace.

In years past, Chapman had learned the nameless passenger to be a reliable source of information. Whenever he needed to know something, real deep background secrets, he called 'the passenger' through a cell phone number and spoke his request into voicemail. Then, after a while, he would receive tickets to a train, a boat or a plane somewhere in the world. On board would be 'the passenger' with the requested information. Or rather: someone who was sent by the passenger, because it was always a different person. Could be a man, could be a woman. Never someone he recognized. Never someone who really knew anything at all; just a messenger who carried an envelope or an e-mail address or any kind of clue.

And Rogus Magnus was working for governments. A detective for hire, sometimes for the United Nations, sometimes for some army or a secret bureau, but always official.

The involvement of officials meant that Chapman had to hurry. Strong arms were interfering with his current mission.

There was too much money involved, the people who hired Chapman in the first place had promised him a huge amount of money for finding something quickly.

The last thing Bruce Chapman needed was a race against a government. The task at hand was complicated enough as it was.

Chapman left the cabin quickly. He looked into the wagon and when he saw no one, stepped out and closed the cabin door.

Within moments he passed the first corridor and walked back towards the dining car.

"I thought you might have changed your mind, Sir," said the waiter, who walked towards him as soon as Chapman arrived at his table. "Shall I carry on?"

"Please, do," said Chapman.

He sat down at his table and took a sip from his wine glass. The turn of events puzzled him. He looked around to see if there was anything out of the ordinary, but there wasn't. The older couple still sat there. In the windows he saw the vague night sky — and his own image reflected in the black glass.

A woman should be looking at that, he thought. *Not me. This is my last job. When this is done I am going to live in the sun with a beautiful woman.*

Faces passed in the night. All the women he knew and had known, but not a single one of them was a suitable candidate for the future Chapman had in mind. Not one of them really knew him. And not one of them was up to the challenge.

Bruce Chapman carried with him, on the train, a life of lies.

Being an assassin for hire had made him independent and wealthy, even to the point that retirement was becoming a serious option. Continuing in this line of work beyond one's fiftieth birthday was a very bad idea. Too many dangers. Too many threats. His profession was for young men, vigorous, trained, aggressive.

Most of the time though, his missions didn't even involve killing. He had moved from the raw working man's business of letting people disappear from the face of the earth to the more sophisticated art of tracking down people or things. Sometimes only to shoot someone at the end, or to steal the wanted object. These days, Bruce Chapman was all about getting information and his current assignment was a good example of this.

All he was required to do, was finding the exact location of the virus that the Everest corporation had developed decades ago, and report that location.

From the file, which he had destroyed after receiving and reading it, Bruce had understood that this virus had incredible powers, and that Everest had also developed an antidote.

Thinking back about this file, Bruce smiled.

These people were ruthless, no doubt about it. What did it matter who owned this virus and this vaccine? They were going to use it to steal from every citizen of the world and pile more money on top of what they already had.

So he had mixed feelings about this assignment.

There's something to be said for an honest criminal, he thought. *They kill people, they sell drugs maybe, but they aren't hypocrites about it. Then there are pharmaceutical companies: they'd take their own mother's last dime in exchange for a pill that does absolutely nothing for her health. Ordinary people spend their last money on medicines they can't afford.*

He was thinking about changing his mind about this assignment. Particularly because there had been a piece in the file about the virus being extremely dangerous, and having been tested in Africa, where it had become known by the name of Ebola.

If these people had a cure for Ebola, then that was the sickest thing Bruce Chapman had ever been involved in. And he had been involved in some serious sick sh**.

In the mirroring window, Bruce saw long forgotten images. Rocked half asleep by the rhythm of the train wheels on the track and the soft lights of the dining car, he let a rush of memories come over him. He was the kind of man who shrugged off the past whenever it showed its face, but he might have been growing tired of holding back. In the safety of the train, with both the men he was supposed to be dealing with out of the way, he allowed himself a weak moment.

In the mirroring window, he saw himself, decades ago in a jazz city, a dreamy image from far away.

There you are, Bruce thought, *walking the pavement.*

The early night. Summer in the city. Sticky asphalt. The air full of ambulances and jazz.

The boy with greased hair stopped somewhere in a park, observing a kissing couple in the vague light of a street lamp. The park was deserted, in a time when city park nights were less dangerous. An audience of stars looked down.

While outside the window dark hulls of mountains passed by, Bruce saw, in his memory's TV screen, the boy bring the girl home and then walk away.

You are not going to kiss my sister again, he thought.

Then the stab and that sight: the boy who had kissed his sister was suddenly lying flat on his back. The blood. The alley.

One thing had changed since then. He remembered killing

his sister's lover with a passionate heart. But he had stopped feeling things like that a long time ago and now all he wanted was to feel like that again; like something *mattered*.

Across the image of the deadly struggle in the city alley appeared images of his father, hovering above the young boy that was Bruce, hammering his fists down.

The dinner table.

The mother: "Tell your father about your history class, Bruce."

The boy: "I was..."

The father: "Shut up. I don't want to hear about it."

The finishing of the dinner, wrapped in silence.

Bruce remembered everything, but none of it mattered.

Ten

With dessert, finally, came a message. After putting coffee and a digestive on the table, the waiter slipped another envelope to Chapman, as unobtrusive as possible.

"I was asked to give you another message with dessert, Sir."

Chapman opened the envelope and read the message inside and smiled.

Seems like I'm getting somewhere, he thought. *Finally.*

He drank the coffee while he read.

"Dear Mr. Chapman, in case something happens to me before I get to speak to you, I have arranged for the information you seek to be stored for you online. Below you will find an email address and the login code. When you log in, go to the inbox and open the only message there. It will contain the location and other specifics."

Chapman put the envelope in his coat and drank the rest of the coffee. A shadow fell over his table.

Chapman looked up. A man stood by his table and looked

down at him. He was older with a pointy mustache and sported a gray suit.

Chapman gestured towards the opposite seat. The man sat down. He threw a card on the table.

It had a government logo on it. *E.M. Rachete* it said. And: *Deputy of Field Security.* Along with a cell phone number and an email address.

"Well, Mr. Rachete, it seems you're a big shot," said Bruce.

He observed the man in front of him. A clean and crisp suit, albeit incredibly boring grayish. A slim man, quite tall, with short brown hair and, in the middle of his face, a large mustache curling up on both sides, crawling across his cheeks.

For a moment, Bruce gazed at the mustache. It was so out of date it was almost unbelievable.

"My friends call me Emmet," said Bruce's table guest. "You can be my friend too. So, what have you found out so far, Chapman?"

"Who wants to know?"

"My government."

"I have nothing that is precious to me. Come to think of it, neither does any government."

"Nice one-liner, Chapman. It's a pity there's no audience to spread the word."

Chapman took a napkin and cleaned his lips. "I have nothing to say. Can't you tell me something amusing? Killed any spies lately?"

"We know the case you're on, we know who hired you. You

will tell us what you know. You must realize you are playing with fire here. National security is at stake."

"Now that's not very nice," said Bruce. "I don't think I want to be your friend anymore."

His table guest smiled. He was not impressed.

"That's not up to you, I'm afraid, Chapman," said Rachete.

"Where I come from, you choose your own friends."

"Not anymore. I happen to be one of the very few people who was allowed to look into your file."

"What's in it?"

"You do stuff for our government and for some other governments and nobody wants to be remembered. I am instructed to get in touch with you, but leave you alone. You are... untouchable."

The last thing I need is politics, Bruce thought. *Rivalry between government bureaus.*

But he said nothing. He looked out the window, starting to feel tired all of a sudden.

"Untouchable, yes..." Rachete continued. "That is: as long as you are working for us. And it seems to me you are not working for us right now."

Finally, Bruce sighed. He no longer felt like hiding his fatigue. "Maybe I am and maybe I ain't. Sometimes I'm hired by a government, *your* government, through an agent. Some corrupt official, who hates your guts, wants to stay out of your sight and your files and hires me through an outsider. Could be the tax office. Could be the army. Who knows?"

"You know."

"I'm not sure. And I don't care."

"Of course you don't care," said Rachete. "As long as you get paid. But I need to know what you know. If you know stuff about Ebola that can save people and you are keeping it to yourself, I swear I am going to make your life miserable, Chapman."

With a smile, Bruce waved the waiter and said: "That's what I like about you people: your trustworthiness."

"Trustworthiness?"

"Yes. You never trust me and you are never grateful. I can always count on that. That's a rare certainty these days, to be able to count on one's employers."

"You are a sarcastic man, Chapman."

"What do you take me for, a moron? I want nothing to do with something like Ebola. I'm just doing my job but you can rest assured I do not want that beautiful file of yours that has my name on it stained with the death of millions."

"It doesn't have your name on it. We know your name is not Chapman. Nor any of the other names you're used to using."

Rachete got up. "I'm sorry you're not ready to share information with me yet. I do understand, you have your own business to run. I just want you to know we're watching you and we will step in at some point. We are not going to let you get away with this secret. So anytime you're ready to bring me on board," —he pointed at the card on the table— "give me a call. Good day, Chapman, or what's your name."

It pleased Bruce that Rachete was clearly annoyed by the

fact that he could not discover his true name. Even after all these years of doing business with governments, they still could figure out who he really was.

However, it did *not* please Bruce to find E.M. Rachete on his tail. He should be working in the shadows, not with one of the world's largest secret agencies in his wake.

"Take care, now," said Chapman, watching the official disappear.

That mustache is a real gem.

Behind him, a few tables away, a woman had taken a seat and looked at Chapman for a moment, but then focused on the menu. She was dressed elaborately, as if she were a gypsy girl about to disembark the train and walk away across the ice fields. Black hair erupted from underneath her woolen bonnet, touching the air around her, as if challenging the world to try and tame it.

She felt Chapman's eyes on her for a moment; in the reflection of one of the windows she could see him as he looked on.

But it was no more than a moment, for all he did was order another coffee and look at the passing landscape; full of thoughts and no interest in a passing lady.

How could she have known that Bruce Chapman locked every face deep inside his memory?

"A new environment can bring a shock. It has been known to lead to a complete change of personality. We humans are only partially ourselves; most of who we are, is made up from the world around us. Change that world, and we change ourselves."

—From the diary of Hitomi Sakamoto

Eleven

Only the most daring guests showed up in the hotel gym before dawn. Brightly lit, it offered the chance of starting the day earlier and making more of it than those who lingered in their beds of silk and satin on the floors above.

For some of them, however, the early rise promised to be quite a challenge. Waking up before your natural clock gives you the OK signal can be quite confusing: the spirit still starting up while the muscles are already working out.

Hitomi Sakamoto, being an early bird all her life, suffered no such setbacks while she practiced her karate movements on a mat placed by the boxing equipment. She was completely at peace with her inner self and went through slow motions to warm herself up without paying even the slightest attention to her surroundings.

The rectangular basement floor was at least forty meters long and twenty meters wide, with a high ceiling bathed in white light. Fitness equipment was spread out in an orderly fashion, and at least ten hotel guests were working out, a trainer among them whispering instructions to an elderly couple. He used a lot of gestures to cross language barriers.

In the distances within her mind, Hitomi saw the karate class of her youth, her teacher Kiyoshiro's features too vague to focus on, and the movements she had practiced ever since. She saw the old courtyard of Kiyoshiro's school and the leaves of the ivy, while at the same time the sweet smell of the sun's empire unwilling to reveal itself once again.

"If you're not practicing boxing, move out of the way, woman," a voice barked close to her.

The images of her youth evaporated.

A hulk of a man stood in front of her, unshaven, dressed in a washed out T-shirt and training pants. A gold chain hung across his chest, tied to a bulky neck. His hairy arms were placed akimbo, an expression of annoyance glued to his square face. His head was bald, but the hair was intent on taking possession of it real soon, a gray shadow emerging.

Hitomi continued her motions, taking her eyes off the intruder again.

"Well?" the man insisted.

In front of his face, Hitomi moved a hand with the grace of a ballet dancer, from left to right, capturing his eyes.

"I'll be done in just a minute," she whispered. "Then you can come back here and practice being a cave man."

Things happened very quickly from that point on. The hotel guest shouted something from his throat, perhaps "bitch!" in some language unknown to Hitomi, and raised two arms towards her in an attempt to push her away, off her mat.

But Hitomi grabbed one of his outstretched arms, turned her body around its center while destroying the man's balance. She bowed down, pulling the arm with her, sending the man across her back into the boxing training machine. Then she stepped back to allow the man to fall to the floor.

Behind them, the instructor and all the hotel guests had stopped what they were doing and looked on.

"That was rather rude," whispered Hitomi. "Now that you've disturbed my concentration, I might as well continue my morning routine somewhere else. You can have the floor."

She turned and walked away towards a training bicycle, stepped on it and started exercising.

In the mirror she saw the man crawl back on his feet, rub his neck, look around him and distribute an angry look among the spectators before he turned to the training machine and started to kick its patches, jumping up and down.

"Can I offer you my compliments, miss?" said a man on the bicycle next to her. "It's not often that one sees someone dealing with rudeness in such a decisive, concise manner."

Hitomi looked up.

My, what a fine example of the tall stranger, she thought. *And he's eloquent too.*

"I'm Bruce Chapman," said the man, stretching out a welcoming hand.

Hitomi shook it. "Hitomi Sakamoto," she said. "Thank you for the compliment."

While she continued her exercise, she felt the eyes of her neighbor on her shoulder. It was part of her routine to absorb any disturbance, so it was all right. For Hitomi, working out was both a sharpening of the body's muscles as well as the mind's.

"It is no use living in a healthy body when the mind can't deal with the world around it," her teacher Kiyoshiro had once said.

True words.

Twelve

The chandeliers hovered over the tables like quiet angels, suspended in the air while pouring their light over the guests of the hotel.

From her table in a corner close by the windows overlooking the frozen city, Hitomi Sakamoto allowed the light to flood her, to warm her, to infiltrate her. Because the destination she had chosen for her vacation, this city on the edge of the Arctic Circle, was in desperate need of more light. Even if it was a yellow light, not nearly as bright as the sun, it bathed the restaurant and made it feel warmer than it actually was.

"Miss Sakamoto?"

The hotel manager stood by her table, making the tiniest bow and an elegant gesture, entirely appropriate for a man wearing a tuxedo, to the man standing next to him. "Please allow me to introduce to you Mr. Chapman, an excellent expert in snow adventure travels. I can vouch for him, but if you need any extra credentials I will be happy to supply them for you." With an additional nod, the sort that could have gone with a clicking of the heels, he turned and walked away between the hundreds of guests at their tables, smiling here, nodding there, like a father to all.

Hitomi nodded as well, towards the other seat at her table.

But Chapman grabbed her hand and put his lips on the back for a remarkable light kiss. Then he sat down gracefully.

For a moment they looked each other in the eye and smiled.

Then they started talking simultaneously — and stop again.

Immediately, Chapman gestured Hitomi to commence.

"Mr. Chapman, meeting you is turning into a habit."

"You don't strike me as a woman who follows any other habit than her own," said Bruce.

"How have you been briefed by the hotel manager, if I may ask?"

This was, in Hitomi's almond eyes, a crucial moment. Her whole plan to take a trip into the arctic wild for a week and ride a dog sleigh and use her beloved Japanese bow and arrows, all depended on this man's response. She knew she could trust the hotel manager because he had the finest references. This was the man to turn to if you needed a reliable guide for a private trip into the snow, into a remote area such as the Arctic lands beyond the city.

It would be just the two of them with the dangers of snow and freezing temperatures, avalanches and cracks in the ice, wolves and polar bears.

He looked good, for starters. She had been observing him in the gym that morning and had concluded he was, indeed, a fine tall stranger.

But Hitomi was not on the lookout for a new boyfriend or a travel companion. She just needed a guide and also a protector, because women might have been liberated in large parts of the world, might have been liberated from a lot of bull's manure since the last witch was burned alive — it was still dangerous to be a woman when you were alone.

"You want to spend a week in the proximity of the boreal forest, preferably away from any tourist route, you do not want the experience to be formulaic, you want to ride a dog sleigh, hunt with a bow and arrow, be safe and not talk unless you have to," said Chapman without smiling. He looked down at his hands while unfolding his napkin and putting it on his lap, and he didn't look her in the eye until he was finished with the talk and his napkin.

"You seem like an accurate man," said Hitomi.

Chapman nodded only once, barely visible.

"You have also taken the liberty of adding that last thing to your briefing. I never instructed them that I didn't want to do any unnecessary talking during the trip. What made you draw that conclusion, Bruce Hillsborough Chapman?"

The man rested both wrists on the table, his hands unfolded, as if he was inviting her. His mouth opened up, but it took a moment for the words to come out.

"You got my whole name, Miss Sakamoto? No one has ever called me that in my entire life."

"Get used to it," said Hitomi.

"I saw you, I saw how you just nodded when we were introduced, and I knew you are not here for small talk. You just don't need it. You are tired of it. Your life is full of small talk and you need to get away from it."

Hitomi looked straight into Chapman's eyes.

In the corner, an ensemble began to play some sonatas by Bach on two violins and a violoncello.

Then the waiter appeared and poured them an appetizer, while explaining the origins of the drink, but they weren't listening.

"That's all right, Miss Hitomi. I have no small talk to offer. Sometimes one has to endure that. I have to, like you do. So I guess we're both lucky we don't need that. Why don't we talk about the landscape you will be traveling through? There's so much to know. There are many dangers to understand. And then there's your bow, of course."

Finally, Hitomi smiled, albeit a modest smile. "Sounds good to me, Bruce Hillsborough Chapman."

And that's how Hitomi and Bruce got off on the right foot. Very convenient if you're about to walk on the tundra — also called the boreal forests — in winter.

"But how do you know about my bow? I told no one."

Chapman drank from his appetizer. "I made that deduction. You're Japanese, you want to be in the wild in winter, without meeting any tourists, you do not want to stay in boring hotels or cabins and so forth. Obviously you want to live off the land for a week, rough it, skip luxury. Making noise in the boreal forest by shooting guns draws too much attention for your taste. So a bow, a traditional Japanese weapon, would make sense. Am I right?"

"Apparently."

"You brought a yumi, didn't you?" said Chapman.

"You're informed," said Hitomi, charmed, although she showed no outward signs of it. "Ever used one?"

"Stopped a bear with a yumi once," said Chapman. He touched his chin with one finger and looked in the distance for a moment. "The environment where you and I will be going requires a series of skills in case we have to engage serious wildlife, like wolves or polar bears. It's important to be able to handle anything, or to be able to make your own weapons."

The waiter took their requests for dinner and hurried off again.

"Are you lecturing me?" said Hitomi. "You don't need to do that, you know. I can protect you if there's a polar bear on our path. It's just that, because I only have one week to spend, I need someone who can help me get there quick and waste no time looking for a place to stay and checking out maps. Your role is to point the way, basically, and take care of logistics."

"I'm a bit of a logistics expert, Miss Sakamoto. Anyway, I like your approach. You don't trust anyone when your safety is on the line. That's good. But you do want to know where we will be on the map in case something happens to me, don't you?"

"I want to know everything, Bruce Hillsborough Chapman.

I want to know everything."

Chapman lifted his glass towards Hitomi. "Here's to a rough trip, then."

"Take it easy, wild man," said Hitomi. "I haven't decided yet."

Thirteen

The room was entirely dark when Bruce Chapman opened it up. Normally he would step right in, touch the switch next to the door and allow soft light to flood his hotel room from several angles. Two fake candles by the bed, a wall lamp above the flat-screen and one lighting part of the floor.

But not this night, for the room was cold. The chill sent him a warning, because it was too late at night for a maid to have been here recently, and the temperature was way below average.

Obviously, a window had been open only moments ago.

So to be on the safe side, Chapman stepped in without switching on any lights and closed the door silently behind him. He stood with his back to the door and allowed his eyes some time to adjust to the darkness.

It's a good thing this is not one of these new hotels where the lights go on automatically when you insert your plastic card in the door lock and step in, he thought.

He didn't think anything else, because his response to an

alert of this kind was fully automated. He reacted almost from his subconscious.

I must not be childish about this, Hitomi thought. I don't have the time for it.

She was laying on her bed a couple of floors lower than Chapman, contemplating the decision ahead. It had been a wonderful dinner, which she had enjoyed more than usual. Considering the fact that Chapman had been selling himself, it was certainly a successful evening. Usually, dinner with someone who has something to sell turns out to be business, which is kind of boring in a way. Hitomi had a talent of compartmentalizing business and pleasure, and sitting through business without expecting it to be too much fun. It didn't have to be fun, for her. But tonight it had been fun, even while this preliminary meeting was business, strictly speaking. It had been all about Chapman showing off his trade, and about Hitomi deciding.

Something inside of her always spoke against business being pleasure. Hitomi had decided to take a trip into the wild with a good guide, but without turning it into a trip of buddies. She didn't like trips with guides who wanted to be your friend. She wanted to enjoy the ride alone, with the guide only there for safety and plotting the course on the map.

From that point of view the evening had not been entirely satisfactory. She had actually enjoyed the company of Bruce Hillsborough Chapman. They had chatted about everything.

He had asked her about her childhood on Hokkaido, of all things. Men never asked about that.

And what's more: she had told him about it.

About the snow and its habit of laying across her childhood like a warm blanket. About the silence it brought. About her grandfather, who had taken care of her after her mother's death, who had taken her to a remote village and taught her about plants and animals you could eat, how you could find and prepare them, how to grow your own food, how to fight and how to be silent, silent like the snow. Within her was always that landscape of mountains and trains in the snow, and the tunnels where the ice and snow could fall off the trains. And most of all, the tiny train station in the mountains, where she would leave and always come back, and the poem that was engraved on the station building, the one that told everything one needed to know about man and snow in a mere three lines.

In the end the evening had been enjoyable, when it should have been merely business.

That confused her.

But Hitomi Sakamoto, being a producer of a business radio show that demanded her utmost, was used to making decisions quick and right. She decided to think about it for another five minutes and then deal with it.

Through the darkness, Chapman moved in the shades of the room. He stayed clear of whatever light came through the curtains — lights from the hotel park lanterns, reflected in the snow — and by the time he was behind the couch he saw a shadow behind a curtain. Someone was standing between the cloth and the glass.

Chapman smiled.

Well, it *did* look ridiculous: someone stood there waiting, expecting the light from within the room to make him invisible. But the light came from outside, exposing the intruder.

When Chapman was close enough to smell the perpetrators breath through the curtain, something stirred behind him and he realized fully that he had made a rookie's mistake. But it was too late to respond, because a heavy body jumped on his back and he was pushed forward, towards the curtains and the shadow he had been watching.

Strong arms grabbed around his throat and started to choke him, while a man's voice shouted behind him: "Stick the needle in him, asshole."

Chapman bent forward with all his might and threw his attacker over his head, into the curtains, right onto the shadowy figure.

Only now did he notice that the door to the terrace was open. The three of them plunged onto the balcony, into the cold night.

With both attackers in front of him in a swirl of curtains, it was easy for Chapman to push through. He knew he had to knock them down before they could use any weapons on him.

In the whole process of pushing through, the man who had jumped on his back, moved over the railing of the balcony, and went over it — and then just hung there, stuck in the curtain with an arm and a leg. The curtain was held back by the weight of the other attacker.

Chapman put his knee on the man's chest and grabbed his face. Even in the pale moonlight, the curtain revealed nothing of his attacker's face.

"Talk now or you go over the side: just say you're innocent. Say it!"

The man mumbled: "In... innocent."

"Nice accent, sucker. Thanks for letting me know."

The gun in Chapman's hand landed on the man's head. He fell back, losing his consciousness immediately. Moments later, Chapman pulled up the other man and delivered the same blow to him. They were now both unconscious. Bruce walked back into the room and took a syringe from his bag. He injected both men. Then he lifted their numb bodies, one by one, and dumped them on the next room's balcony, beyond the aluminum screen. Both bodies fell down with a thud.

There was not a drop of sweat on Bruce's face. Nor was there anything else visible on his face; he did the work mechanically.

After closing the balcony door, Chapman turned on the lights and hung the curtain back on its rail. Apparently it had not been torn, so when it was in place again, no one would notice the difference.

He took out a cell phone and dialed a number.

"Everest is on my tail. Just got rid of an assassination team. No, they're alive, they'll wake up in a few hours. Dead bodies will draw attention of local authorities and I don't need that... Yeah, well, consider it a mantra... No, I'm out of here. I need to vanish now, before they find out and send new material... I just know. One of these guys had an accent like a neon sign. No doubt about it. I'll be off line until I am close enough. Make sure your team is ready to move in... No sooner than forty-eight hours from now. There will be a radio silence, you can't contact me until I am ready."

Fourteen

With unusual poetic flair, Carreidas looked out the window and thought: *I am not a scientist. I am a failed alchemist and my heart is as frozen as this landscape.*

The only real fact in this thought was the landscape: it stretched outside as far as the eye could see and there was nothing but snow and ice. He stood standing in a concrete room in a concrete building. The fluorescent light was painfully white and sounds were echoed a thousand times, but the temperature and humidity were pleasant and the place was full of more than adequate technology. There were old-fashioned paintings on the wall, socialist visualizations of an imaginary workers' paradise. There was a full metal desk with a leather chair that he could sit in for days without ever getting into physical trouble. There were computer monitors and additional screens. Somewhere in the hull of this building, Carreidas had his private living quarters, a comfortable living room with a kitchen, a bedroom and a bathroom.

But to Carreidas it all felt as cold as the arctic landscape outside. And just as deserted.

In these parts, people hardly ever showed up. There was the occasional hunter. Or sometimes a few tourists, usually a small group of rich people being led through the wilderness by a guide, hoping to shoot a moose. They never caused problems because the outside of the building was uninviting; it was dull and almost without windows, and there were several *no trespassing* signs on the outside. His bosses had paid off the government, so there was no harassment from officials — not that there were any. This was one of those regions where no one caused any trouble. Lack of troubles is very convenient for officials. It means they can look the other way.

I've looked the other way for decades, Carreidas thought. *Looking away from the shame and the pain.*

By now he felt that he paid a heavy price for a mistake he made when he was a young man.

I was blinded by ambition.

It had been youthful enthusiasm and ambition that had driven him into the greedy hands of the Everest owners. After all these years he thought of Lord Rand and Locarn as ordinary crooks. But back in the days, young Carreidas had been intoxicated with the thought of fame and glory.

Like Van Hagen, another sucker for fame and riches.

Carreidas had also been pushed in the wrong direction by his older colleague, his mentor, Professor Van Hagen. A charming man with a very persuasive streak. What they had been doing in Africa, testing that virus, was the worst scientific experiment he could think of. Somewhere along the line of the invention of the atomic bomb and the experimenting on twins by Nazi doctors in the Second World War.

But by the time Carreidas had started to doubt, it had been too late. The people of Everest had exerted enormous pressure on him. Lord Rand and Locarn, along with their band of bandits, had created a situation where everything could be blamed on Carreidas if the public ever found out.

"All the records, everything there is, points to you and Van Hagen," they had told him years ago when he had spoken to them about his doubts. "You can do whatever you like, but you can never talk about it. Find the vaccine and you can be a rich man and buy your own island in the tropics."

And since Van Hagen had retired years ago, and had vanished into a haze of dementia, Carreidas was now alone, facing the dark deeds of his youth.

He was never a total prisoner; occasionally he went out with the security helicopter and visit the city of his birth. But he had no friends there anymore, no relatives. He had also neglected his professional network.

Talking about isolation.

There was one other accomplice: Julianna, his laboratory assistant. But she was either part of the Everest board conspirators or entirely without remorse. Carreidas had brought up the subject a couple of times. When Ebola hit Africa hard, years after their initial tests, he had asked her how she felt, and she had simply waved away everything.

"We are scientists, Carreidas," she had said. "You worry too much. There will be epidemics, like the black plague in medieval Europe. Now we have a plague in our hands, to study."

He had persisted and carried on the argument.

But Julianna had ways to silence him that rendered him defenseless. She had invited him to her apartment in the concrete building, and had simply fed him some serious booze and had danced for him.

She makes me forget.

Carreidas smiled for a moment.

It's pointless. I can't make up my mind.

All in all, he was a confused man and he knew it. Whenever remorse popped up, it would be pushed out of him by the cold, by looking away, by the smile of a woman.

It's too late to get out.

"Confusion is an essential part of life. Without confusion there is no doubt about the status quo, which is then destined to remain unchanged. Confusion shakes up the foundations of our faith and allow us to write the next chapter."

—From the diary of Hitomi Sakamoto

Fifteen

Failing to persuade Bruce Chapman had not improved E.M. Rachete's mood nor his confidence in his assignment. Years of low profile investigations had led to suspicion about a certain division of Everest Inc. and its possible involvement in the Ebola virus, but it never materialized. If there was a single man capable of bringing the whole investigation moving again, it must have been Bruce Chapman.

But the bastard was unwilling to cooperate.

Too bad.

Then again, it was probably not the end of it. Although that didn't really enhance Rachete's job satisfaction. To let off some steam, he moved his fist.

The table was in the way of the fist, and so it should be.

The collision between tropical hardwood and human flesh and bones was unmistakable: E.M. Rachete rammed the table three times before he started to speak. Those three punches made his young colleague shiver and think of pain for a moment. Coffee cups bounced. A glass of water fell and shattered on the floor.

For an old man he's sure still got the fire, the younger man thought.

He looked at his senior. The ridiculous points at both ends of his mustache curled up along his cheeks in an otherwise unremarkable face. The gray suit was clean and crisp, as usual.

The young man, however, was dressed entirely unofficial, in jeans and a white T-shirt, his sneakers nervously tapping the floor, his hair in a studied wet look across his forehead.

"Portugal was once a great nation," said Rachete as he started to pace the room.

There was hardly anything in the room; just a table and some chairs, a water cooler by the window, an air conditioner and a modernist painting in a cheap frame, presenting a landscape of squares. The walls were as gray as Rachete's suit, or the daylight outside.

"They had colonies. They sailed the seven seas. They conquered. By the beginning of the twenty-first century they were practically bankrupt, a third world nation in the European Union." He turned to the young man. "You see, young Mr. Willem Brook?"

Brook pointed at him with a finger. "Portugal: check," he said. "I'm just not sure what that has to do with Bruce Chapman and Everest Pharmaceuticals."

Again Rachete turned to the table and hammered it three times. "I'm not talking about them, I'm talking about our Service," he barked. "It's going to the dogs. Don't you see the analogy? We used to know everything. We knew when Stalin was going to the John. We knew when Gadafi was farting. We knew when Saddam was posing for a statue. Hell, we even knew that the French president had an illegitimate child and that Armstrong was cheating on the Tour. And now... Now we can't even tell what a simple commercial enterprise is doing in its laboratory and why it has shipped out something in a hurry and where it is now and why several people have vanished."

"Chapman knows," said the young man. "Check."

"Check sh**," said Rachete. "We don't know that. All we know is he has already been attacked by assassins twice, which means he is closer to the secret than we are."

"I'm arranging satellite vision," said Brook. "By tomorrow morning we can look at him from outer space and stay on his tail."

"We'd better," growled Rachete. "Because the guys up there are getting very nervous. If it is indeed Ebola they're working on, we need to know where it is."

"Can't they just talk to the Everest CEO?" said Brook. "Or arrest the whole board, for that matter."

"We don't want to scare them just yet. We want to know what they have before they find out we know anything. People get nervous when the army moves in, you know. They're in it for the money. Besides, if they're doing something very dangerous, they may fear the law and deny everything. Let's just wait and see. We don't move until we know *precisely* where the virus is."

"Check," said Willem Brook, and he got up and left the room.

Finally, E.M. Rachete got around to getting the glass of water from the cooler. He walked to it and looked down when he heard the cracking of the broken drinking glass on the floor.

He thought of it as a sign, but he wasn't sure if it was a good one, or just very bad.

"You can't expect life to knock on the door from the other side, my grandfather said today. I remember rays of sunlight on his face, playing through the bonsai trees in the courtyard. He also said: maybe it is you who should be knocking on the door, because life is waiting for you on the other side. I will cherish this outlook on life forever. Just jerk open that door and get on with it."

—From the diary of Hitomi Sakamoto

Sixteen

Hitomi strode towards the door, having made up her mind, opened it up swiftly and faced Bruce Chapman. He stood there with his hand raised, ready to knock.

"Let's do it," she said.

"Great," said Chapman, as he walked right in. "Because I just got the weather forecast and there is a five-day window of opportunity near the Arctic Circle. If we fly there now, we'll be in the snow before noon tomorrow. Get your bag and meet me in the lobby in fifteen minutes while I go back and call my pilot. OK?"

"I like a man who is on the move," said Hitomi. "So, what are you standing around for in my room?"

"I need to check your gear," said Bruce.

"Are you doubting my assessment of a trip in the arctic region, Mr. Bruce Hillsborough Chapman?"

Chapman had turned and now stood very close to Hitomi. It was impossible for her to ignore his physical closeness.

"If I'm going to be responsible for your safety I must check your gear," said Chapman. "I don't know you, I don't know your history, I can't take your word for it. Besides, where we're going, there's no extra gear. You got the wrong shoes and you're doomed. We're going to rough it, remember? So, show me your gear."

"It's over there," said Hitomi, pointing behind Chapman.

He turned, but while he did that, Hitomi grabbed his arm, pulled it, turned, bend over — and her newly hired arctic guide flew over her head to the floor.

"Might as well start to rough it right here and right now," said Hitomi.

Before he knew it, her knee was in his throat.

"That is the first and the last time that you doubt my word, OK? You can check my gear, if it makes you feel good, but that's enough. I pay you to be my guide, not my guardian."

Chapman smiled. When Hitomi removed the knee and he could speak again, he said: "I offer to take your gear for granted, Miss Hitomi Sakamoto."

Part III

Seventeen

Hitomi looked out the window of the bungalow. The whole southern side of the house was made of glass, from the ground up to the roof, and it looked out downwards across an ice and snow covered plain, some twenty meters below. The whiteness of it was stunning. In the distance, mountains reached for the sky, their vertical slopes of dark rock standing out in the snow. Parts of the landscape in the distance were covered by a boreal forest, thin, but thick and dark.

Next to the fireplace behind her, a framed map of the region was pinned to the wall. It showed a vast territory in a vertical rectangle, starting at the bottom with the plains, then mountains and the boreal forest in the middle, and finally the start of the Arctic Circle at the top.

The house Hitomi stood in was located in the middle of the map, in the part where the mountains began and the boreal forest creeped across the plains and the hillsides. There was not a single building or road marked on the entire map, except for a railroad that lay dozens of kilometers away.

She had arrived here earlier that day, jumping from the small airplane Bruce Chapman had hired. Three parachutes had sailed down to the slope that surrounded the bungalow: one for Hitomi, one for Bruce and one for a large crate containing their gear. The cargo parachute had come down first, to prevent possible danger, and while she was suspended in the air, Hitomi had looked down and noticed the splendid isolation of the house. It gave her a chill to think they would be in a place away from all people, just her and her guide, in the middle of the wild.

They had made a soft landing in the snow and spent the next hour getting the crate onto a sleigh and into the house. In the late afternoon they had rested and taken a bath. Finally, Bruce Chapman cooked a dinner in the open kitchen while Hitomi looked out across the plain.

There had been a remarkable ease between them from the beginning, she thought in the silence of the house.

Hitomi realized that Bruce had not, like most men she knew in the city where she worked, put on the radio first thing upon arrival. Neither of them needed the noise of music in this majestic landscape. The silence that was forced by the snow upon the land outside was also omnipresent in the house, and they both embraced that as something natural.

A unique quality in a modern man, she thought.

She heard some soft sounds coming from the kitchen dresser and immediately concluded that the good man was indeed preparing sushi. No other dish sounded like that; the vague whisper of the seaweed paper, the soft clicking of the knife separating the portions. The faint smell of the rice had prepared her for this.

"I am not going to ask you who this house belongs to," said Hitomi, when the two of them were sitting at the table overlooking the snow fields.

"Of course not," said Bruce. "I wouldn't want to start a boring conversation about some billionaire, who had this built out of sheer boredom and has never actually stayed here. It's much more interesting to discuss why you want to get away from everything, from your job at the radio, and what you plan to shoot with your bow."

"I brought it for self-defense in case you do turn out to be a sociopath," said Hitomi. "But my radio station job, well, there's really nothing interesting to tell. I produce a business talk radio show that runs five nights a week and has ten million listeners worldwide. I like to think I contributed to that, but who can tell?"

"Who indeed."

"You are really the odd man here, who's interesting to talk about," said Hitomi. "You are not a regular wildlife-guide, you are much too sophisticated for that."

"My parents were rich. So I can pretty much do with my time as I please. Most of the time I hang around in Monte Carlo and places like that, but I need the excitement of a tour of duty like this. It's full of danger, you know. There can be severe snow storms here. It takes practice to be a good guide and organize a safe trip. I'm not sure about the bow though.

Can you handle it properly?"

"You are really not doubting my abilities, Bruce Hillsborough Chapman, said Hitomi, while she sipped some sake.

"No, I am not."

They ate sushi and drank sake and looked at each other for a while without talking.

"In fact, I am puzzled by it," said Bruce. "I have seen some Olympic cracks shooting the bow, tall women from, I don't know, the Ukraine or Canada. But never a small Japanese woman who is not in her twenties."

"So it's new to you?"

"Yes."

"You'll get used to it," said Hitomi. And then, after a pause: "Until you get bored by it, eventually, like all men do."

Abruptly, Bruce stopped his hand before it could put the sushi slice into his mouth, and put it down again. "Yes, I get bored so fast you can hear me break the sound barrier."

Then he got up, verified the vague hint of a smile on Hitomi's face, left the table satisfied and walked over to the grand piano to play some Bach.

Hitomi sat back and drank the music.

This could be intoxicating, she thought. *All this.*

"Only when one is away from the noise of the deadline, it becomes possible to be one's self. In the absence of the usual, the forgotten becomes visible again, like a friend who has been away for a long time, remains a friend."

—From the diary of Hitomi Sakamoto

Eighteen

The white was unlike Hitomi remembered. The light was different here than it had been in her snowbound childhood days. Much closer to the North Pole, it seemed paler, and it lasted longer during the day.

Ahead of her, Bruce Chapman rushed his snowmobile with a daring speed, leaving behind a white cloud. Hitomi had a tough time keeping up with him, bouncing across small hills, feeling like she was plowing through the white dust. They were moving upwards on a slope, which started naked at the bottom but became covered with trees slowly as they moved up. The thick pine trees stood dark and straight in the shadow of their canopy of snow. Before long, they were zigzagging between the pine trees and forced to slow down a bit. But not much — Bruce kept pushing the limits and there were moments when Hitomi almost hit one of the thin trunks.

When they arrived close to the top of the hill, they dismounted.

"This is a good place to test your bow," said Bruce. "See if you can capture a small animal for tonight's dinner. You up to that?"

"You bet," said Hitomi. "Expect hare for the roast."

"I'll walk on to the top, I want to see how the view is up there. We meet back here by the snowmobiles in forty-five minutes, or one hour at most."

And off he went.

Hitomi took the bow from her back and took a couple of arrows from her backpack on the snowmobile. Then she set off, away from the machines, but staying on the same altitude.

Within twenty meters, she spotted a hare, quickly laid the arrow on the bow and shot. The arrow plunged into a tree right above the animal. It looked around and hopped away.

Hitomi smiled. She had intentionally aimed above her prey. She had decided to respect the peace that ruled over this country.

We can eat something from our supplies, she thought.

===

"Aim above the animal, into the tree," whispered Hitomi's grandfather.

"Why?" little Hitomi whispered back.

The bow was too big for her. Handling it had been tough for her and now that she was finally ready for the kill, she was disappointed.

"It means us no harm and we don't need food now. It's just practice. It's just a way of respecting nature."

"I need to know if I can hit it accurately," Hitomi complained. "What will I learn from missing it?"

"You will learn," her grandfather hissed in her ear, "what you are ready for."

===

On top of the hill, Chapman took out his electronic binoculars and searched the horizon of the snowfield below. Every few seconds he looked around, down the hill, through the trees, to make sure Hitomi didn't see him.

In the distance stood a dark structure.

Chapman looked at it for a while. Then he put his binoculars away and sighed.

Nineteen

Clown, Julianne thought.

She looked at Carreidas, the scientist working on a virus of unprecedented power, yet looking like a funny professor from the movies. It was normal for a scientist to make mistakes, because that's how science moves forward: through trial and error. But Carreidas would blush whenever something went wrong, and be embarrassed about it. After that, he would bicker endlessly with her about the reasons for the failure.

She couldn't make up her mind. Was Carreidas just bantering or was he being dead serious? There was simply no way to tell. Even after all those years of working with him.

Julianne was the laboratory assistant, thirtyish, hiding her beauty behind a mask of seemingly clumsy glasses and a laboratory coat. Carreidas knew what she could look like because he had seen her outside working hours. But in this white facility he seemed not to notice, as if the artificial veil around her beauty was an unwritten contract that allowed him to focus on the job at hand.

For three years they had been in this building now. Ever since Van Hagen had left there had been just the two of them working in the middle of nowhere. They worked with utmost secrecy in the white laboratory zone, surrounded by nothing but a few guards. These anonymous men took care of security, but since they were surrounded by an empty landscape with a hundred kilometer radius, they were mainly occupied with logistics. Food was flown in by helicopter to the courtyard of this strange, prison-like facility.

Literally speaking, it was not a prison; the scientist and his assistant left for the weekends, when they both led a relatively normal life a couple of hours away by helicopter. They both left for longer periods too, to have a vacation, but never simultaneously.

The test animals were the only ones who never left.

In fact it had been a government building, built here half a century ago to investigate the climate of the North Pole. Because of the Cold War in those days, the walls were high and plastered white, the whole thing built close to a white mountain to hide from sight. Behind the building was the safety of the rocks, in front of it no one could approach it without being seen.

On top of that, it was large. Around the courtyard, the size of a soccer field, the three stories of the building rose from the snow, hiding endless corridors and rooms and laboratories and storage facilities in the basement. She had lost her way here more than once.

Since the discovery of the virus a couple of decades ago, the Everest corporation had created the mother of all secret operations: keeping the origins unknown while searching for a medicine that would one day be strong enough to make a fortune. From the onset, it was clear to the management and the scientists that this thing called Ebola had not been contained. It was large in the 1970s, and for a couple of times in the decades since it reared its ugly head.

Only six people in the whole world knew that Ebola had been invented, albeit unintentionally, and then tested and thus exposed to the world, by Everest scientists. Those six people were Julianne herself, Carreidas, Van Hagen, Lord Rand, Locarn and Burlow.

Everone else had met his or her expiration date. A corrupt military chief in Africa, plus some of his men, had been ambushed and killed by some guerillas who were paid handsomely. Two lab assistants who had been unhappy with their knowledge and had been having second thoughts, had been sent on vacation to think things over and had never returned.

None of the other people involved knew exactly what it was that Carreidas and his assistant were working on in that bright laboratory.

Not the security people who had been taking care of the remote laboratory all these years.

Not the families of Julianne, or Carreidas, or anyone else.

By then, even Everest's highest official was kept out of it.

As far as Julianne was concerned, one had to be willing to sacrifice a lot for science. She felt lucky to be in the position to nurture the future medicine for something as horrible as Ebola.

The fact that Ebola was conjured up by the same corporation she worked for, many years before she got into the profession, was no more than a rumor to her. All she knew was what she was told. That other companies and governments might want to steal their knowledge and that the origins of the virus were vague. That it had been a mistake. And that the testing in Africa; well, that had been a mistake but the people responsible were long dead and if word got out, you would get a public panic and all that.

Fortunately, Julianne was a practical scientist who was only interested in the medicine and its miraculous powers. She tended to the bio-cultures in the laboratory, five days a week.

It never bored her. In the evenings she caught up with reading, because she wanted to grow in her field.

There was one thing that bored her sometimes, and that was Carreidas. Or bothered, to be more precise.

"I can't focus when we are quarreling," said Julianne.

Carreidas sighed. "Focus on what, Julianne?"

There, thought Julianne. He's making a fool out of me. He hasn't been serious for a minute.

But that was about to change.

"I do not believe for one minute that your hypothesis is even worth writing down," said Julianne.

"The pressure from the corporation is finally getting to

you," sneered Carreidas. "Poor woman."

"Who cares about Everest? There are more important things at stake than shareholders' value and future profits. This goes back to the discovery of penicillin. For all I know we are at the brink of a new era."

"An era of utter destruction, if we're not careful."

Julianne raised her arms and sighed. "Now you doubt us. Now you tell me about your second thoughts. Great. We're in the middle of things, we can't back out now."

"Don't put words in my mouth," said Carreidas. "I'm only challenging your hypothesis that the antidote is as stable as the virus."

"You..." said Julianne, her face flushing suddenly, "you prefer to destroy the virus, don't you?"

"I'm just saying there's no proof yet," said Carreidas. "Perhaps Everest's expectations are unrealistic and the decision should be postponed."

"Bollocks."

Carreidas walked over to the glass chamber in the middle of the laboratory. All its walls, including the ceiling, were made of the thick, double layers of glass. The inside was full of wires and tubes, and a chimpanzee was tied to a stretcher. The animal was quiet, as if it was sedated.

"I don't need any more proof."

He pressed a button.

Inside the glass cage a hydraulic robot arm moved down and injected the animal.

It started to shake and bleed from its eyes and nose.

The scientists looked on without expressions on their faces, as if they'd forgotten their argument instantly.

Carreidas pushed another button and a spray was released inside the cage, like a fog emanating from invisible nozzles.

When the fog lifted, the bleeding had stopped and the chimpanzee turned its head in their direction, nodding as if approving their actions, the blood clotting around its eyes and nose.

Carreidas sighed.

Julianne said: "I don't need to see this again. You've made your point, Carreidas." She gave him a look that hit him like a punishment.

"Sorry," said Carreidas.

She controls me, thought Carreidas. *I am a wet towel of a man, I have a girl to rule me. If Van Hagen had still been here, he would have laughed at me.*

Then he sneered at Julianne: "We will repeat this test as often as we like. Without at least a hundred tests, we have achieved nothing. If your stomach isn't up to it, you can face the opposite direction. For heaven's sake, woman, it's only two seconds before the antidote is released."

Carreidas walked away. "I am not going to do another eighty tests on animals," he said. And then, louder: "Release the ape, please, Julianne. I'm going to ask for human subjects."

Twenty

For a long time the daylight seemed to be held prisoner by the endless white landscape. Even after the sun had vanished beyond the horizon there was still light, a fading reflection of the day that was slowly replaced by the upcoming shimmering from the stars. Hitomi felt like a voyager in a zone without time, where the twilight was stretched in both directions. She almost regretted arriving at the bungalow.

She would come to regret it, but for an entirely different reason.

Hitomi and Bruce drove the snowmobiles under the carport, just in case it would start to snow again. Stepping off, taking off their ski glasses and their hoods and their mittens, they stood there for a moment, observing one another for signs of fatigue.

"Ready to lie down yet?" said Bruce, his face not betraying whether this was an expression of concern or sarcasm.

Probably neither, thought Hitomi. *He's a man who knows precisely what to say and when to say it, but conjured up in a practical mind.*

Proof of this, she thought, was the fact that Bruce Hillsborough Chapman — in spite of being an adventurous man with a shroud of exciting secrecy about his life, a man of the world and a man who knows how to survive in wilderness and a women's world — had an almost undetectable tendency towards the cliché. This heroic image of him, his tall, handsome looks, his athletic build, functioned as a cover up.

And Hitomi Sakamoto was the kind of woman who found it impossible not to see through this — even though she appreciated this kind of man. Not necessarily a *true* man; in her work she needed to assess people quickly and correctly, so that the radio show she produced would never be compromised. On live radio, one needed guests you could depend on.

She had a lot to find out about Bruce, about who he was. But for now, all she said was: "I was born ready, not lying down."

A nice mixture of the cliché and the original, Hitomi. Well done.

By that time Hitomi and Bruce left the carport and entered through the front door.

The moment they stepped inside, lights were switched on and three intruders were revealed.

All three of them pointed a gun at them.

One barrel touched Hitomi's left temple.

One barrel touched Bruce's right temple.

The third gun pointed towards them from halfway in the

room.

"I'm tempted to say freeze," said the man in the middle of the room, "but I don't want to overdo it."

He was a thin man, with fluffy curls rolling down his parka. He looked pale, fragile, but his dark eyes were piercing between two old-fashioned whiskers.

"Please be seated."

Hitomi and Bruce started to walk towards the couch at the other end of the living room.

"But tread carefully."

The guns' muzzles stayed pressed to their temples until they reached the couch and sat down.

Facing the three barrels, Bruce said: "Anything we can help you lady and gentlemen with?"

"We'll be asking the questions," said the thin man. He put the gun away and took off his parka.

The other man was of the type that's hard to define. He was as average looking as they get, except for a big black mustache that sat on his face as if someone had used a marker to give him at least *one* distinguishing feature.

But it was the woman that drew Bruce's attention.

I've seen that face before, he thought.

The thin man and the man with the mustache stood in front of them, their guns pointed at their faces. The woman sat down at the table and took a piece of paper out of her parka, put it on the table, and looked at it intently.

Even though Bruce's face gave nothing away, Hitomi could sense that whatever was going on, and whatever these people were doing here, it had to do with her travel guide. She noticed how he looked longer at the woman than he looked at the men — a fraction of a moment longer, perhaps.

You better not be imagining things, Hitomi Sakamoto. Or grandpa will get his whip. His verbal whip that was, of course. His tongue could be razor sharp.

And it was indeed so that Bruce realized he had seen the woman, just like that, sitting on the train. The black hair erupted from underneath her snowcap just the way he remembered. He also remembered her gypsy clothing, her radiant presence in the train's restaurant. At the same instant he realized that hiding any of this for Hitomi was coming to an end.

"We need you to tell us the precise location of the virus," said the woman, looking up. "We know you know, Mr. Bruce Chapman."

"You are confusing me with someone else, obviously," said Bruce with a burst of laughter that sounded more like a gasp.

Hitomi looked at him in utter confusion. The three invaders looked at each other.

"That's a nice logo you guys are wearing," said Bruce, pointing at a round emblem on the woman's parka. The emblem showed an illustration of Earth, with green continents in a red ocean, plus the words 'Eco Warriors'. "Seems like you guys are on a mission to save the planet. We sympathize, and we're no threat."

The woman answered in the iciest fashion imaginable. "We may be on an honest quest, but we are willing to use force, Mr.

Chapman. To make sure we don't lose any time, we can give you an example that will urge you to comply. Go ahead, boys."

The two men lurched forward. Hitomi and Bruce were grabbed and pulled up from the couch, both of them facing the barrel of a gun.

Twenty-one

The blade was as cold as ice. Hitomi shivered when the knife pressed against her skin.

Bruce watched on, ice water running through his veins, moving upwards across his back. Unexpectedly, the danger now threatening his temporary employer, Miss Sakamoto, was deeply upsetting. Had he really grown to like her in that short time? Since when had he started to feel fear again?

Under normal circumstances he wouldn't have cared. Collateral damage was to be expected in his line of business. But he worried about the outcome of all his, about the effects of the knife and the guns. He thought about his own weapons, out of sight, in his bag. He had been prepared to proceed with his plan, fully armed, when the time was right, and had not anticipated a raid at their base camp. He felt unprepared.

He looked at the woman in front of him and at the gun she pointed at the map on the table between them.

Hitomi was held from behind by the mustached man. He was simply too strong for her to resist. Her arms were folded on her back. The skinny guy had jerked at her clothes, opening up her fur coat, moving her sweater and shirt upwards and now pressed the knife against her left breast. Hitomi could feel the blade's sharpness.

"This is not a negotiation, Mr. Chapman," said the woman. "Show us the location now or my friend will start to strip your friend of her dignity." She paused and smiled. "And of the rest of her too."

"Fine," said Bruce. He bent over the table.

"Careful," warned the woman.

Bruce let his fingers run along a latitude and longitude, then let it slide into the white openness in between the lines and hammered the map… *somewhere.* "There."

"There's nothing there," said the woman.

The thin man moved the knife a bit and Hitomi uttered a sigh.

"The building's not on the map," said Bruce. "Isn't that obvious? It's still there. Here, I'll mark it for you. Take us along if you don't trust me."

Environmental activists, he thought. *That's not going to help.*

The woman took out a device that could be a smart phone, typed something on it and said: "There's a building there all right. You better be right, Mr. Chapman, because we'll be coming back for you. OK, lock them up."

The thin man put away his knife and the man with the mustache let Hitomi go, so she could draw her shirt and sweater down again. So far, she had refrained from speaking. Both she and Bruce had behaved withdrawn and had shown no anger or resistance.

They were escorted into a utility room in the back of the house, a place full of stuff. Canned food, petrol, every kind of gear you might need in this cold landscape, from snow shoes to goggles and skis. In one corner stood the central heater; the rest of the walls were filled with shelves. There was food for a year.

The thin man was taking his time tying them up.

"Hurry up, man, we need to get there before dawn," said the mustache.

"This needs to be done with precision," said the thin man. "Don't you ever watch movies? You see them escape all the time."

"Who cares?"

"That's because the tying up is done in a rush," said the thin man. "It's important to..."

"What are you guys up to anyway?" said Bruce.

But that was right before a cloth was shoved into his mouth and sealed with duct tape.

Twenty-two

For a moment, Bruce was feeling lucky. The first thing he saw when he woke up was Hitomi, freeing one of her hands from the rope that tied them to her back.

The first thing the hand did was rip the duct tape from her mouth. She coughed out the cloth.

Hitomi then showed Bruce the hand in the half-light of the utility room and did so with amazing grace. Bruce watched as the hand rose vertically, the index finger pointing upwards and the little finger floating horizontally, and the other fingers in between, the whole hand opening up like a Chinese fan, the thumb drawing a mysterious circle.

"See that?" said Hitomi.

Still duct taped into silence, Bruce shrugged.

Hitomi slapped Bruce's face with such force, that his head twisted backwards, against one of the shelves. A series of food cans fell down on him.

"This is the hand that will torment you," said Hitomi. "Until you tell me what you know that you haven't told me."

She proceeded by freeing her other hand, then got up, jumped around on her tied legs until she found a knife on one of the shelves, which she used to cut through the rope around her ankles.

Bruce had been expecting a swift release, but he was disappointed.

Hitomi slapped his face four more times, banging him against the shelf behind him. Only then did she remove the duct tape from his mouth, with a painful jerk.

"Sakamoto, will you knock it off!"

"Bruce Hillsborough Chapman," hissed Hitomi, "don't you play the innocent choirboy with me. You have put me in a dangerous situation and you have done so knowingly. I resent that. From now on I will distrust you. Live with it. Now tell me what you know or I'm going to dance on your face."

Hitomi rose and lifted one foot in front of Bruce's face. "I mean it. I can do without your bullshit anytime."

"We're a thousand kilometers from nowhere, Sakamoto. You need m..."

Before he could finish the sentence, Hitomi pushed Bruce over. He fell flat on the floor, hands and ankles tied, and got Hitomi's snow boot on the side of his face. And she pushed real hard.

"Talk to me Chapman."

Then she bent over, grabbed his hair and slammed his head to the concrete floor.

"Alright!" he screamed.

Hitomi backed off and leaned against a shelf, massaging

her wrists.

"The Everest corporation has discovered a very deadly virus by accident," said Bruce. "They have hidden it in a secret location in the ice and are probably studying it, or storing it, or working on a vaccine. The world's most powerful government is on their trail. I work for a competitor of Everest. They paid me to steal the virus."

"Why?" said Hitomi. "What's the value?"

"In today's weapon market a virus can be priceless. Same thing goes for a vaccine."

"It's illegal and it's dangerous. Not even the stupidest dictator will use a virus," said Hitomi.

"Well, then they can sell it to their government, who wants to control it or destroy it or keep it out of the hands of dictators or religious fanatics or criminals," said Bruce, his voice beginning to show irritation. "And if it's true, if they've really found a functioning medicine, it is vital that it is protected by the right people and doesn't remain in the hands of a few crazy corporate schmucks. Either way, it doesn't matter, Sakamoto. It's worth a lot of money to a lot of people."

"Then what are they waiting for?"

"They can sell it when it's ready, I guess," said Bruce. "Listen, that's all I know. My job is to locate the virus, that's all. Now will you, please, be so kind as to untie me?"

Hitomi walked around, looking on the shelves until she found something. She returned with a crowbar and put it down on the floor before starting to free Bruce. "From now on we work as a team," she said. "Promise me that and I'll untie you."

"I promise."

"Don't think for a minute that I believe you, Bruce Hillsborough Chapman," she said. "As far as I'm concerned you are a walking lie and you have put me in danger without any consideration for my safety. I will remember that."

Rubbing his painful wrists, Bruce got up from the cold concrete floor. "Want to hit me one more time to drive home your point?"

A corner of Hitomi's mouth moved in a hint of a smile, but it was hidden from Bruce.

It lasted very short, then she turned towards the door.

"Listen, I'll volunteer some more information, just to prove myself to you," said Bruce. "The virus that Everest discovered, or created, all those years ago, is now known as the Ebola virus."

By that time, Hitomi was using the crowbar on the door. "Don't get any ideas, Chapman. I like you. I also don't trust you. Until further notice, I consider the idea of Ebola having been conjured up by man utterly ridiculous."

Bruce put his arms around Hitomi and grabbed the crowbar. Together they forced the door out of its hinges.

"Thank you," said Hitomi. "Just remember your promise to work as a team from now on."

The house was deserted, the white plain abandoned outside the windows.

"They've put us to sleep with that injection for at least four hours," said Bruce. "They have probably raided that location and took the virus or destroyed it or whatever. Too bad."

Hitomi looked through the glass wall.

"Listen," said Bruce, "I have to go there and see if I can still finish my job. Go after them. The people who pay me are not going to be very forgiving if I turn up empty handed."

"I'm coming with you," said Hitomi. "That virus should be in the hands of the government, not some creepy corporation and not a couple of mentally unstable environmental activists."

She started walking to the front door of the house, stealing a quick kiss from Bruce while passing. "If it wasn't for your job, we could've been taking it easy in this bungalow, enjoying a lazy afternoon." Then she vanished into the outdoors.

"These people are armed and dangerous," said Bruce, following her into the snow. "Doesn't that bother you?"

"I'll bring my bow," said Hitomi. "You bring your own stuff."

What does she know about my arms, thought Chapman. *Perhaps this woman appears more innocent than she really is. Perhaps she checked out my luggage and knows the score.*

While he joined Hitomi by the snowmobiles, he thought: *It doesn't matter. If she gets in the way of my job, I can get rid of her.*

Just to make sure, when she looked at him, he gave her a fake look of a man who's interested. He gave her a faint smile, full of innuendo.

Even while he did that, Bruce Chapman contemplated killing her on the spot. But only for a moment.

He decided against it for practical reasons. *The woman's good in a fight,* he thought. *You never know.*

"We better hurry," he said.

He checked his bags, which were still tied to one of the snowmobiles. No one had touched them and he felt relieved. He touched the bags. Felt the packages of explosives, the guns.

Twenty-three

The forest was a roof of snow that rested on logs. From within its darkness Hitomi and Bruce looked across the white plain. In the distance, a helicopter crossed the plain.

"The facility was used as an observatory during the Cold War," said Bruce. "I'm not sure what it was built for originally. It's not on any map. The Everest Corporation bought it after the Berlin Wall was brought down and the Soviet system collapsed and everybody thought there would be no more threats. They supposedly use it to work on medicine. Because of the cold and the remoteness of the place it is pretty secure. I've traced them. They brought the virus here. It's just that I couldn't get to it just like that. I needed to look like a traveler. You and me needed to look like travelers. Two people travelling through the snow, that way, I thought, I could get close."

"What about the helicopter?" said Hitomi.

"They fly people in and out all the time. The scientists who work there, stay only during work days. On weekends, all the staff is replaced temporarily. It's a weird outfit as far as I'm concerned. One of these scientists has been working there for decades now, can you imagine that? Listen, if you take out your binoculars you may be able to spot the place. Or those Eco Warriors."

Hitomi did just that and saw a dark structure against a mountain backdrop.

"It's covered in the back by the mountains," she said.

"Not necessarily," said Bruce. "There's also a rift in the ice-field, between the building and the mountain. Can you see it?"

"I can see a shade, that could be it."

"In theory," said Bruce, "we should be able to travel to the other side of the forest, lower ourselves into that rift and get to the basement of the building without being noticed."

"Aren't they watching in every direction?"

"Getting to that rift is very difficult," said Bruce, "so I honestly don't think they'll be expecting visitors from that direction."

Hitomi gave him a stern look.

"Don't worry," he said. "You're the athletic type, you can handle it."

"Don't make up stories," said Hitomi. "Just give me the facts."

"OK lady, you asked for it. We need to spend the night in the forest, then climb down on the other side into an abyss, and then walk through that rift to the building. The bottom may be frozen or wet, whatever."

Those are facts I can check easily, thought Hitomi.
But she decided to stay alert nonetheless.

Twenty-four

They weren't alone in the forest that night.

There was a wolf on their trail.

"It doesn't bother me," said Hitomi.

"It bothers me," said Bruce. "Now it's one wolf. Next thing you know it's a pack. I'd feel safer if we killed it before it makes any noise."

"Nonsense," said Hitomi. "We're not going to harm wildlife without a good reason."

"Says the hunter. Didn't you bring your bow and arrows for some good sport?"

"Not wolves. Get the tent. It's really getting too cold to stand here and argue."

So they put up that tiny polar tent, a circular piece of synthetics, its flaps clapping in the wind while they were busy.

When they crawled in, Bruce said: "So you've put up this type of tent before."

"This is not my first trip in the wild with a primitive man," said Hitomi.

Then she said "Now be quiet" and started to kiss him.

"We... we can only... sleep for one hour," muttered Bruce. "We need to be there before..."

"Before dawn, yes," said Hitomi. "One hour will do just fine."

Hitomi zipped two sleeping bags together to create one. "That way we can combine body heat," she explained.

Her face was in the shadows of the flash light lying on the ground behind her, so Bruce couldn't tell if she smiled or not. But if he had any doubts about what Hitomi was really saying, they were taken away as soon as he was in the double sleeping bag. Hitomi's hand was on his buttocks before he got a chance to lie down on them.

"Do warriors abstain before they go to battle or do they not? That is the question," said Hitomi.

"What's your position on this?" asked Bruce.

"That is such a superfluous reply, Bruce Hillsborough Chapman," said Hitomi, as she moved her body on top of his. "I expect more from you."

"Such as?"

She whispered in his ear, barely loud enough for him to hear above the hissing and howling wind outside. "I expect you to rise to the occasion."

After a while, Bruce had to get out of the tent to take a leak. He crawled out, got up on his feet, walked about twenty steps through the trees, feeling the trunks and branches with his hands in the pitch black and finally unzipped.

He felt a great relief.

Then there was a growl. A soft, low pitched sound, coming from right in front of him.

He saw two tiny lights.

In an instant, Bruce decided to continue what he was doing to make sure the animal in front of him would not be stirred by a sudden change of events. He slid one hand into his trousers and took out his pocket light.

As soon as he had finished his business and zipped up without making a sound, he switched on the light. The sudden reflection of all that whiteness surrounding him, blinded him momentarily — all he could see was a dark shadow jumping towards him.

Only then did he realize that his gun was in the tent.

"My grandfather told me about the war today. In the distance, the city burned. The buildings around him were mostly rubble. Everybody fought everybody, if not for the war itself it was for food.

Grandfather went out with his bow and arrow and was taken by the soldiers. He was still very young, a mere boy. The soldiers kept him with them, for protection. But it was the soldiers who needed protection. Because when they came under fire by a sniper, he crawled around buildings and shot an arrow through the sniper's arm."

—From the diary of Hitomi Sakamoto

Twenty-five

The arrow hissed past Bruce and stopped the wolf in mid-air. The animal fell before his feet without uttering a single sound.

"Bruce Hillsborough Chapman," said Hitomi, appearing out of the darkness behind him and stepping into the light, "we need to stay focused here. We don't have the resources to battle stupidity as well. Come back in the tent."

"You think that's the only wolf?"

"Does it matter? I'll protect you. Just don't use your gun as it draws attention."

The wind had upped the ante by the time they folded the tent into a package and started to move the next morning. As if millions of snowflakes had formed a razor blade while they were sleeping, and were now attacking them.

Bruce dug up to goggles for protection.

"Shouldn't we wait out this storm?" shouted Hitomi, through the noise of the flapping tent.

"No. This is the best. No one will see us coming in this weather."

But that was also the only benefit; everything else combined to a serious downside.

Visibility was down to zero. All they had were the headlights of the snowmobiles and a compass. The snow threatened to separate them. And ahead of them, somewhere, the forest would end and lead them down into a small abyss.

So they skied slowly, but not slowly enough. Suddenly the ground disappeared from underneath Bruce's headlights. It was too late to come to a halt, so he threw himself aside and drew the snowmobile with him; the machine toppled and when Hitomi crashed her mobile into his, the trip came to a full stop.

"Wonderful timing!" shouted Bruce.

But Hitomi gestured him to shut up. "Lights off, quickly," she hissed.

The storm slowed down quickly and visibility restored. A pale moon shone through the clouds, showing them what Bruce had called "the abyss": not much more than a crack in the icy landscape, a shaft of perhaps ten to twenty meters deep at the foot of the mountains. On the left were the white plains, on the right were the slopes.

Bruce pointed in the distance. There were vague lights.

"That's the Everest building, no doubt," said Bruce. "Let's push the mobiles back into the forest to keep them out of view. Then we can start climbing down."

Hitomi looked at the walls of ice leading down, raised her

eyebrows and then turned to help her travel-guide achieve his next short term goal.

Twenty-six

The path Bruce had chosen was a dangerous one. They had to climb down along a wall of rocks and ice. Slipping or losing grip would lead to a deadly fall. The only good thing about this part of their quest was that this crevice in the landscape was rather shallow, fifteen meters at most. Still, the fall would be long enough for them to break every bone in their bodies or die, so they experienced a few awkward moments.

Like the one when Hitomi slipped and was rescued only by the strong grip that Bruce had with both his hands: one on the protruding rock he held on to, and the other one around Hitomi's wrist.

"Your reaction time is admirable," sighed Hitomi after he had lifted her back up to a point where she could stand on something and hold on.

"There's no guarantee," said Bruce. "Please don't slip again, I may miss you the next time."

By the time they arrived on the crevice's floor, a few minutes later, Hitomi had decided that this life saving action meant that Bruce was to be trusted.

But she didn't feel the need to share that with him, so she looked away towards the direction they were headed.

"You cover my back, I cover yours," whispered Bruce. "Listen, I know I had a hidden agenda, but I want to get you out of this snow in one piece. You are not part of my mission."

He checked his backpack. Then they started to walk the crevice floor towards the Everest building.

"I hear a river," said Hitomi after a while.

"That's not possible," said Bruce. "There's no river here."

But he was wrong; within moments they were standing at the edge of a fast flowing stream. Apparently it followed an underground trajectory and crossed the bottom of the crevice. It came out of the side of the crevice and disappeared into the other side, creating a tough barrier for them to cross. It was no more than three meters across, but it was too much to jump on this slippery bottom. It was too cold and wild to wade through.

"We have to climb up a bit again," said Bruce. "But be careful. If you hit the water, this stream will suck you underground. Not good for your health."

They both tied a rope around their waists. Bruce climbed two meters up the side and started to cross the river, while Hitomi held his rope. He reached the other side safely and then took Hitomi's rope in his hands and waited for her to climb the same route.

When Hitomi was right above the stream, a rumbling noise sounded, and a large piece of ice broke off from underneath her feet. She hung down from her two hands.

Below her, the piece of ice was squashed into little fragments that all disappeared underground quickly, into the stream.

"I'm going to swing," said Hitomi. "Make sure you catch me, I do not want to get a wet suit in this cold!"

It took her about sixteen swings before she dared to let go and fly through the air on top of Bruce. He captured her, although he collapsed to the ground with her in his arms.

They waited for a moment to see if any more shards of ice were going to break off or if anyone had heard them, but nothing happened. Hitomi got up and gave Bruce two hands to help him get up as well.

They were now only fifty meters from the building. It rose high above them like a dark medieval castle: a black shadow disappearing into the snowy air above them, a towering, colorless power, hiding its evils within its silence.

Twenty-seven

Ten minutes later they were standing at the foot of the building.

The crevice through the landscape cut right alongside the foundations of the building. There was a large circular opening, shielded by thick metal bars. A green, greasy slime covered the bottom of it.

Some small birch trees had sprouted here, along with some low bushes. Bruce seemed to know what he was doing: he pushed the bushes aside and revealed a wooden door. He lifted his backpack to the ground, took out a metal contraption that held the middle ground between a pocket knife and a key, messed around with it for a moment and opened up the door. While it swung open inwards, he looked back at Hitomi with a smile.

"I don't believe in coincidences," he whispered.

"Neither do I," Hitomi whispered back. "Although I do believe in stupidity."

That remark took Chapman by surprise. He stood frozen

while Hitomi passed him, stepping inside the buildings cellars. "Stupidity?"

"Why build a fortress like this and then put in a kindergarten door in the basement?" said Hitomi.

They were inside. From the first moment on, it was clear that the basement of the building had been neglected for a very long time. It was damp and messy, and their flashlights stumbled upon endless rows of abandoned crates and building equipment. It was nothing more than a series of concrete walls supporting the building, without any doors to create separate spaces. On the ceiling were lamps and wires, but they didn't switch anything on.

Bruce showed Hitomi a floor plan.

"We're here. Over there are the stairs. We must get to the third floor, that is the most likely place for the bacteria to be stored in their freezer. The experiments must be on the fourth floor."

"How many people will there be?"

"They are working with the smallest crew possible, just the bare minimum to keep the operation going. They figure the less people know about it, the safer their secret is. So we'll find a laboratory staff of two, if I'm correct, and maybe two guards, not counting visitors that come in by helicopter every day or every few days, for checkups or meetings or supplies."

They decided to take the ladder inside the maintenance shaft; a cylinder than ran vertically through the building and contained everything from ventilators and electricity and water and heating pipes to a tiny emergency ladder.

Twenty-eight

Obviously it's not a good idea to scream when you're climbing secretly through a shaft in a building that you're not supposed to be in. But sometimes you just can't help yourself.

It happened when the metal step under Bruce's foot gave way in a cloud of rust, he almost lost his balance and for a moment hung by one hand, while Hitomi first got the full weight of the metal step on her hand and was then kicked on the head by one of Bruce's boots.

"Be quiet," hissed Hitomi, but that was just a waste of breath.

The metal step clink-clank-clunked all the way down into the shaft and Bruce's shout echoed after it.

Within moments, a maintenance door opened and two uniformed men stepped on the platform right above them. Flashlights beamed down and that was that. Automatic rifles pointed towards Hitomi and Bruce and harsh voices barked instructions.

"Get up!"

"Move"

"Great. More activists."

"Keep your hands above your heads. Way above!"

Of course they couldn't put their hands above their heads while they were climbing, so no one pursued the matter.

As soon as they reached the platform, Bruce was robbed of his backpack. Hitomi lost her bow and arrows. Then they were pushed out of the shaft with considerable force.

"It doesn't matter," said Julianne. "People from the corporation will be here tomorrow to take care of these activist hippies and they can deal with these two as well."

"I find it worrisome that this building is attacked twice in just a couple of hours," said Carreidas. "What else can we expect? Anyway, we are not equipped to imprison people. It may create legal problems with the local authorities."

"Local? There are no locals within five hundred kilometers. The authorities have been bought off properly. You seem to forget that you are not only responsible for finding the golden key to this virus, you are also responsible for its safety."

"The corporation should deal with this. How can we be safe with only two guards?"

"They are sending a whole army right now. By morning, we are in good hands. Right now, these intruders are locked up. All the doors are sealed. Concentrate on your task, Carreidas. We are but hours away from the final stage of your research. Or have you lost confidence and are these disturbances nothing more than welcome distractions from the imminent scientific failure you are anticipating?"

Carreidas didn't respond to his assistant's aggressive approach. "You talked to the corporation about this? They are coming?"

"Yes they are. They are on the way and will arrive first thing in the morning to deal with all this. They'll get rid of these intruders and probably relocate us. I mean, if a couple of hippie activists can find us, so can terrorists and governments and we wouldn't want that, now would we?"

They focused on the enlarged images of bacteria on the screens in front of them.

Twenty-nine

"So we meet again," said the woman with the gypsy hair. She looked with contempt as Hitomi and Bruce stood in the room adjusting their eyes to the half-light.

They had been pushed inside the utility room by the uniformed guards, without their possessions: Bruce's backpack and Hitomi's bow and arrows. Now they were facing the three Eco Warriors again.

"Nice of you to come and try to rescue us," said the thin man. "Welcome to our modest prison."

"Very funny," said Bruce. "It seems to me the security here is minimal and in spite of that we all get caught within moments after arrival. What's wrong with this picture?"

"Maybe they knew we were coming and maybe they knew you were coming." The woman moved closer to Bruce and looked him deep in the eyes, with a dark fury radiating from her face, from the dark eyes and the curls. "You stay away from this virus," she said. "We are on a mission to rescue mankind from a mistake and I am not letting you get in our way."

"You environmentalists are all the same," said Bruce. "You'd destroy mankind's greatest discovery just as a matter of principle."

"A man made virus that can wipe out millions of people is not a great discovery."

"It's just a step towards something bigger. Don't you see: a virus that possesses this kind of power can lead us to a new cure, a new generation of penicillin perhaps."

"Enough," said Hitomi, putting her fist between their faces. "We need to find a way out."

The woman looked at her with the same contempt as before. "If I need a fashion statement, I'll ask for it, Mrs. Tourist."

Hitomi moved one corner of her mouth up by almost a millimeter, winked at Bruce and then made a short series of movements with practically every available limb, at the end of which the Eco Warrior woman was on the floor.

Face down.

Hitomi's knee on her spine.

"Shut up, bitch. I said: we need to find a way out. We are in the same building with a group of mad scientists. Better hurry up."

When they were all standing again, the thin Eco Warrior scraped his throat. "I think the lady is right," he said. "We may all want to work together for the moment. We are in the hands of ruthless people. And I don't mean the scientist. I mean the Everest Corporation. Scientists merely search on, they follow a passion, whereas..."

"Yeah, alright," said the third Eco Warrior, the man with the undistinguishing features and the mustache. "There's just one thing I need to make clear hear, Mrs. whoever. We are the Eco Warriors and we are concerned with getting this super virus out of the hands of a greedy corporation, people who are willing to sacrifice everything for profit. We will then turn it over to the government. In case we end up in a situation where you have to choose sides, I think you should know that your Mr. Chapman here is working for the competition. He is in it for the money."

Hitomi gave him her blank face of disinterest.

"If he gets his hands on the bacteria, we're still in trouble."

Bruce moved forward, staring down the mustache. "Meet the benign Eco Warriors, world famous for their benevolence, ready to rush their latest conquest to the government, who hates their guts so much they've incarcerated half of their members and even shot some."

"Those are all misunderstandings," said the woman. She turned to Hitomi and stretched her hand. "I agree we should work together for now. I'm Rachelle."

Hitomi sighed and shook the hand without changing the disinterested look on her face. "Hitomi. Who are your mates?"

Rachelle shook her black curls and pointed to the thin man. "That's Horatio." Then the mustache. "And Forsythe."

"Funny," said Bruce, "how a member of the Eco Warriors, who are known for their violence and their treacherous tactics, goes by the name of Forsythe, which means 'honest man'."

"Would you like me to spill some beans about you to your partner here, Mr. Chapman?" said the mustached Forsythe with a big smile.

"Well, now that we're all friends, let's get on with it," said Hitomi. "Will someone please lift me up?"

She pointed at a grill in the ceiling right above her head. It was located in a corner of the room.

Both Forsythe and Bruce stepped forward. They looked at each other for a moment and then they both folded their hands together to create a step for Hitomi to stand on.

Hitomi stepped into the men's folded hand palms and allowed them to lift her up quickly. As soon as she reached the ceiling, she pushed out the grill, grabbed the edges and looked up into the darkness.

"I'm the only one thin enough to crawl through that shaft," she said, looking down.

Rachelle looked around her. "Why is everybody looking at my biceps all of a sudden?"

"Size matters," said Forsythe. "Ain't that a bitch."

"I can fit through there," said Horatio, "I'm thin."

"Not as thin as she you're not," bitched Rachelle.

By that time Hitomi was already up and gone through the opening. "I'll come back and open the door," she said.

Then she put the grill back in its place and it was all quiet.

"She's quite the athlete," said Rachelle. "Too bad you dragged her into this. Is she your girlfriend?"

"No, she's actually a client."

"Bullsh**," said Forsythe. "Do you have to lie about *everything*?"

"It's always an option to volunteer to be quiet," said Chapman, "before someone punches your mouth shut."

"When the world around me is dark and there is complete silence, I can finally hear the beating of my own heart."

—From the diary of Hitomi Sakamoto

Thirty

The ventilation shaft was not built for human traffic. It allowed Hitomi no room to move her arms from the position above her head. She had to crawl like a snake: by moving her body in waves from her fingertips all the way down to her toes. It was a good thing Hitomi wasn't afraid of confined spaces. This was not a place to contemplate getting stuck.

The shaft went horizontally between the ceiling and the floor above. For a while there was no light. The only sounds she could hear came from far away. Perhaps a door slammed shut, or some industrial apparatus was being operated, or a helicopter moved in the distance.

While she crawled through the darkness, Hitomi devised a strategy in her head. It was clear that she didn't have enough knowledge about the building to go running around. It was imperative that she found the way back to the others and set them free before doing anything else.

Time was on her side. Their captors had left them there only minutes ago and weren't likely to return immediately.

She could be free of this tunnel within moments, find her way one floor down and perhaps pick up a tool on the way.

That was it. There was nothing else to go on; no information about impending dangers or guards or cameras. There was nothing else to think about while she crawled in her snakelike movements, sliding around corners tight enough to get stuck in. Moving into dead ends and having to retrace her movements backwards. And then through the same corners again. So her thoughts drifted off, almost automatically, to that time in the mountains when her grandfather had her climb into a hole in the mountain to catch a fox cub. She didn't remember the reason for the hunt, she just remembered the darkness and the voice of grandfather, whispering in the semi darkness, a comforting wisdom that engulfed her.

"The darkness and the small space you crawl through, change nothing. You are still the same body, you are still the same soul. The air and the sun are no different. The soil embraces you now like the air always does, and the darkness lightens your path like the sun does, but it is a light meant for your fingers, not your eyes. You see: other people are tricked into panic when they are in the dark or when they are in a small space. But you and I know that it is all an illusion: nothing is different."

Every now and then Hitomi passed another grill below her. She looked into them again and again, but never liked what she saw. It was always a corridor with too much light.

At one point, a man in a uniform ran below her and she had

to stop crawling for a moment, until he had disappeared again.

Finally, she looked down through another grill and saw a toilet. Someone had left the lights on; a bright white glow from a luminescent tube. She waited there for a while and when there were no sounds she removed the grill and started the complicated crawl out of the confined tunnel.

Hitomi slid out of the tube headfirst. Like a snake she moved, curled her body while holding on to the ceiling with both hands, moving the rest of her body downwards by sheer muscle power.

Finally, when she hung vertically from the ceiling, she lowered herself onto the toilet and stepped to the floor.

She left the grill where it was and opened the door a few centimeters and look out into the corridor. She remembered the route she had taken and knew that getting back to the door that locked in Bruce and the Eco Warriors was a matter of meters and cutting one single corner.

After crossing the corridor quietly, Hitomi found the door open. The utility room where she had been imprisoned was now empty.

Wherever they took Bruce and the Eco Warriors, they will be looking for me still.

From now on, Hitomi would be looking for them too.

Wait, she thought, *I better get my bow and arrows first.*

She had left them behind in the basement of the Facility. Too bad. This was all going to take some time.

Thirty-one

The scanning tube embraced Bruce's body like a straightjacket. Anybody with even mild claustrophobia would flip out, but Bruce remained calm. He concentrated on the voices he heard. It rose above the soft hum of the scanning equipment only vaguely. But for a man used to solving puzzles it was more a challenge than a nuisance.

Shards of conversation came through, but Bruce had no trouble filling in the blank parts and creating a complete log of events in his head.

"This one is probably the best specimen. Perfect health. A non-smoker. A moderate drinker. An athletic build and an excellent condition. Who is this guy?"

"The top brass say he's been searching to locate our Facility for a couple of years. Finally made it through. He was sent by the competition, basically an industrial spy."

"Well, he can test the goods personally now."

"I'm very uncomfortable with all this human testing. Why does everybody seem to think we will get away with this forever?"

"These people don't know who we are, they don't know what we are testing on them and after being sick for a while they will simply be glad to have survived. Then they will be dumped two thousand kilometers from here and this Facility will be empty before they can talk to a soul. You worry too much."

"What if one of them dies?"

"For crying out loud, Carreidas, don't you trust your own work by now? You have singlehandedly grown the most important vaccine in the history of mankind, tested it on a thousand animals and you still have doubts. You're so insecure."

Bruce tried not to smile at that last remark. In his head he molded the information into something that made sense. Carreidas… not a name that rang any bells.

How can a scientist have worked on the vaccine for three decades and still be entirely unknown?

"Give it to him."

Thirty-two

Only half-conscious, Bruce underwent the medical 'procedure' in a blur. By the time he was transported out of the room to a new location, he was completely gone, off into a gray fog of a dream.

Bruce stumbled through an alley.

He remembered the alley. He had been here before. It hadn't been exactly the same though; stuff had been moved around. He wasn't sure if that container had been here before, or that rusty car. One thing he knew: it had never been this dark. He saw only shades of the walls, of the objects in the alley, and finally, of the boys who were waiting for him.

They were in front of him and they were behind him.

He couldn't remember the leader's name, but he remembered the rest of him. His black leather jacket, his army boots, his crew cut and how muscular he was. Even if none of those features were clearly visible now.

And Bruce certainly remembered the boy standing there like a prisoner, his head down. The boy was younger than the others. He was a classmate of Bruce.

"You want to walk this way home, you have to have permission from us," said the leader.

"He doesn't have permission, Danny," some other boy said. "Can we go beat him up now?"

"No," said the leader. "He's going to earn his permission. Why beat up a perfectly suitable member for our gang? I invite you to join us, Bruce. But this is the last time I ask you. You show us your allegiance. Rough up this classmate of yours and you're free to use these streets from now on."

He saw knuckle dusters appear. One boy started to hit the palm of his left hand with his right hand fist. Others followed his example. He saw even a baseball bat.

A pale moon broke through some clouds momentarily, and Bruce saw the horror in the eyes of his classmate, and then it was dark again, even darker than before — and then he felt himself hurled on top of the classmate and the sweat and heat of the boy's body, and the fists in his face, and how his own fists bombarded his victim and how a heat rose in his head. He saw knives flashing when the moon broke through again, and a tiny Swiss army knife being plunged into his upper left arm —

— and then when he woke, his forehead wet with sweat and the thud of a headache echoing inside, Bruce immediately felt that he had been injected in his left arm. It was the typical sore spot, instantly recognizable from all the tropical disease shots he had had through the years. He didn't remember passing out.

He did remember the dream though, a vivid monster still walking the walls around him for a few moments, but quickly fading. He sighed with relief when this ghost from the past abandoned him once again.

He was in a small, long room. The walls were metal and the place smelled like a zoo. There were no windows, only a door made entirely out of thick glass. Above him was a ventilation inlet.

They took us out of the utility room to this place, thought Bruce. *But why did I pass out?*

He felt the back of his head and then he remembered: he had put up a fight when these guards were pushing him into this cage. Then they had held him down and someone in a white doctor's suit had come in and injected him.

It was impossible to tell day from night. It was even impossible to tell whether he was still in the same building. Past and present had crossed paths and caused a temporary disorientation.

Bruce tried to focus on sound while he looked through the glass door. There was a corridor, apparently, with many more small metal rooms. He saw nothing move through the glass doors on the opposite side of the corridor. Was that a body lying in that one? It was too dark.

He did hear sounds though. Someone was shouting. It could be *help, help*. It could also be shouts of pain, or the noise someone made while having a nightmare. It was the sound of a man with fever, no doubt.

The noise increased. After a while he could determine the

direction and he recognized one of the Eco Warriors' voices. He didn't doubt that this person was in pain, and growing desperate, and weakening as well.

What if they're testing the virus on us, Bruce thought. *Could that really be?*

The thought made him shiver. He had calculated all sorts of developments. He had a Plan B and a Plan C. He had plans all the way up to a Plan Z. He had his tracks covered. He had focus. He had the determination. He considered himself to be the Man with the Plan. But he had been too distant about the virus he had been sent here to appropriate; he had never thought about close contact, about the virus being a weapon *already.*

How stupid of you. Walk in here like a choirboy with your eyes wide open and yet see nothing, hear nothing.

If he had been injected with the virus, would he be able to warn his employers? And if so, would they get there in time?

You must send off some kind of signal. Fast.

But the metal was fused seamlessly and the glass door didn't even have hinges.

The screaming got worse. If it wasn't someone getting really sick, it was someone being tortured severely.

He felt his forehead. The sweat and the heat had vanished with the bad dream.

Funny how you can wake up out of a bad dream, only to find yourself awake inside a nightmare.

Finally, Bruce remembered Hitomi.

She may be my only shot.

Thirty-three

The ventilation openings in the utility room allowed Hitomi to keep an eye on the progression of time. The sun was setting rapidly across the snow fields, and the noise in the building — an engine, someone shouting, the rattling of crates or metal objects, elevators going up and down — started to subside.

However eerie the affairs being conducted in this building's interior, there was a certain routine reminiscent of normal life. Through the corridor she could smell food from some kitchen, along with the metal sounds of cooking gear. After a while, all of that faded too and a silence set in, giving Hitomi the courage to move around and look for Bruce.

Why don't you just get out of here and leave him? She thought. *He is nothing but a liar. Every next hour spent with Bruce Hillsborough Chapman brings you closer to a fatality of sorts.*

She was convinced that virtually nothing about Bruce was what it seemed. It would be prudent to double check everything and take nothing for granted.

You are a sucker for adventure.

One of these days this addiction was going to do her in.

Nevertheless, she stuck with her plan. She was not going to abandon Bruce just because he was a liar. She was not sure about the Eco Warriors though.

And part of her was curious about the news story she was involved in. If only ten percent of what Bruce or the Eco Warriors were talking about was true, then the virus-medicine locked in the interior of this building was going to astonish the world. Even during her holidays, Hitomi Sakamoto remained a radio producer at heart, with a profound love for important news. And a nose, for that matter.

I'm the only one here who thinks of this as a news story.

Hitomi inspected her bow and arrows. Everything was in working order. It was a strange thought that no one had bothered to lock up her weapons. She felt like an abandoned human being, not entirely alone in the world, but yet entirely invisible.

The corridors were now only half-lit. Someone had decided that there was no threat and therefore the normal night procedures could be followed. The good side of this was that Hitomi could move through the corridors faster and more relaxed. At some point, she heard an elevator and then, suddenly, the lights above her returned to their normal illumination.

Someone is coming out of the elevator and the lights are turned up automatically, thought Hitomi.

Hitomi quickly withdrew from the corridor and took shelter in another utility room. She heard two men pass by.

"I want this whole test to be over with within twenty-four hours. I do not like the steps these scientists are taking. They're playing god now."

"We have an official go from Everest."

"I don't care. We're crossing a line. As soon as any of these guinea pigs starts to show signs of deterioration, it's over and done with. They get the vaccine on the double."

The voices faded until they were gone and the lights were turned down again.

Hitomi went back into the corridor towards the elevators.

Thirty-four

Carreidas lay on his bed. He stared at the ceiling and tried to focus. But his thoughts meandered through him, out of control, which was not so bad. After concentrating for a whole day it was nice to let it go for a while.

It occurred to him that for the first time in quite a while he had been thinking about his assistant Julianna as someone other than a scientist. They had had the good fortune to have fulfilling lives outside of the Facility. If they had been two lonely scientists, things would have been difficult because Carreidas was a classical man, he was convinced that relationships in the working place should be avoided at all times.

But every now and then, when the day had been very productive and he felt comfortable about their collaboration, he could become confused when he looked into her eyes, or stood close to her and felt her warmth, or smelled her sweetness.

Those moments passed quickly, he knew, but it could

occupy his mind for a short time. In the morning it would be forgotten, but he allowed himself this vague longing for a while.

She is crazy, he thought.

Then again, so was everybody else involved in this insane experiment.

It takes a certain kind of madness to go this far. Perhaps she is crazier than I am and therefore she is oblivious to my male charms.

Not that Carreidas thought of himself as a charmer; but still, the solitude of this place and the work were the perfect conditions for a romance. Two people a thousand miles from the world clinging to one another.

But she had never given even the slightest hint of being interested in him. For all he knew, she was doing it with one of the guards. She said she studied in the evenings, but he had never seen proof of it.

There were more mysteries here, to Carreidas. He knew very little about Julianna. She might as well be a spy for the Everest top brass. Why not? Someone had to keep an eye on whatever Carreidas was doing. Not the guards, the nameless men in black who roamed around the building and patrolled the perimeter. They just kept everybody out and everybody in. No, the only person to watch him closely and assess what results he was getting, was Julianna.

He had thought this many times before since the sudden leave of absence of Van Hagen: what is the Everest corporation up to anyway?

They must be spying on me.

He had felt that all these years.

They must be spying on me.

But he never got proof of that. The Everest bosses accepted his every word about the progress of the medicine. Every now and then they came over for a visit and emphasized this: "Do not speak to anyone. Have you spoken to anyone?"

Carreidas would always say "no" and they would believe him.

He shook his thoughts off his mind.

Carreidas was never going to say anything to anybody about the Ebola virus and the medicine because he felt he had nothing to gain. He had spent all these years in relative solitude finding the most important vaccine of the past millennium. That was the only thing that mattered: to complete the work and then start producing the vaccine in large quantities. It no longer mattered to him that they had threatened him into secrecy, that they held such power over him.

The vaccine was going to save millions of people.

It no longer mattered that the Ebola virus originated from the Everest labs as well. Not to him it didn't.

But there was always this doubt.

They are going to kill you as soon as the antidote has been proven to succeed.

That was why, earlier that day, he had decided to use these intruders as guinea pigs. By now, too many people knew about what was going on. It was getting harder and harder for

Everest to keep things a secret the way they were going.

Typical, he thought, *how quickly both Julianna and security had agreed to go along with this. These people are ruthless.*

His own ruthlessness meant nothing to Carreidas. Science had nested into his cells; he didn't doubt his own actions for a millisecond. But the actions of others always puzzled him. In that sense he was a true scientist: curious about everything and everybody, except his own motives.

He lay still on his bed. The drastic decision he had made earlier that day, to use real people in the testing process, had stirred something deep inside him. Part of him resisted the direction he was going in; another part reveled in it, really enjoyed it, and somehow brought more darkness to the surface: suddenly he found himself imagining Julianne's soft hands on his back, the beginning of a wonderful massage...

Massage?

Then he felt someone sit on his back and it was not Julianna.

Carreidas turned his head and stared into the tip of an arrow. Beyond it was a large Japanese bow. It was vibrating with tension.

A Japanese woman had stretched the bow, pointing right at his face.

"Talk softly now," she said, "but very fast."

"About what?"

The Japanese woman moved quickly and shot the arrow right into the bathroom door. It ripped through Carreidas' white laboratory coat that hung there.

"Notice the perforation of the heart zone," whispered the woman in his ear, swiftly replacing the shot arrow with a new one on her bow. "Try again."

There and then, Carreidas remembered that the security men had been searching for a missing visitor. He had forgotten about that. How careless of him.

"They're all down in the animal testing area," said Carreidas. "They've been injected with a virus. So... freeing them and taking them out of this place right now is a very, very bad idea."

"Not if you cough up the antidote, doctor," whispered Hitomi. "Now, I'm getting off you, but don't let that give you any funny ideas."

Thirty-five

Lord Rand expressed his feelings serenely as ever when he said: "If this wine is a taste of things to come, we are in serious trouble, my friend Locarn."

It was true: the wine didn't taste good, neither did any of the food. Perhaps they were just distracted.

Rand and Locarn sat at the table at the Palais Corinth and ate quietly for a while.

"We need to assert our position," said Locarn. "There is no doubt in my mind that imprisoning a bunch of eco fanatics is the dumbest thing Carreidas could have done."

"Carreidas didn't do that. Your security people did that. Besides, I approved it."

"Using them as guinea pigs is what I'm talking about. These people are unforgiving. It is also highly unlikely that they are operating on their own. Other people will come look for them. And then this other man, he's an outsider. What's his name again?"

"Let me see. B.H. Chapman. The B I don't know. The H

stands for… Hillsborough."

"Chapman, yes. Who is he working for? It could be a government for all I know. Or worse: *the* government."

"You worry too much," said Lord Rand, putting another slice of beef and some lettuce on his plate. "I do believe that the wine goes best with the lettuce. Swallow it with lettuce, I say."

"I don't see how we can worry too much. We can worry too little. Never too much."

"You are mistaken, my friend. This is not a philosophical debate, this is merely a chat about logistics we're having. It's too remote for any party to make swift moves," said Lord Rand in his usual serene way. There were no ups and downs in his voice, ever. "Just send in a squad, evacuate the virus and the vaccine and all the paperwork, give everybody a vaccine shot, send them onto a glacier somewhere and take off. No one will ever know anything."

Locarn's mouth fell open. "My my, you have quite an appetite tonight, Lord Rand. Whence the sudden blood thirst?"

"Don't talk as if it's anything new. I just feel that you can't wait any longer. Whether Carreidas is ready or not, everything your people tell you is proof that we are moving towards a next phase. There are too many people sticking their nose into the Facility. We must make our move."

He swallowed some beef. "Your people can clean the place up in no time, I know. I'm just worried about how these eco lunatics found the location. After all these years of secrecy, someone must have talked. Do you think Carreidas has gotten to an outsider?"

"No," grinned Locarn. "I have someone on top of him, as a matter of speaking. He's completely dedicated to science."

"Get rid of him," said Lord Rand. "I'm tired of you torturing a scientist into submission for so long."

"Oh but he was all too glad to go along for most of the time," barked Locarn. "He has the biggest ego. He wanted to be in the history books. You know, as in 'Fleming discovered penicillin'? He wants to be in the annals as 'Carreidas who discovered the cure for Ebola'. He was eagerly infecting people in Africa back then and he was very eager to inject these visitors to do the final test. He had to do a final test sooner or later anyhow. I am not torturing the man. He's torturing himself for all I know."

"I don't trust him. You know, this whole operation will go down the drain if anyone talks. Get rid of him while you still can and get the vaccine onto the market through our regular laboratory."

"After these visitors have been cured by the vaccine of course. If they die, people will come looking for them."

Lord Rand sighed, which made Locarn look up in surprise.

The man never sighs.

"It has to stop."

"Getting cold feet, my lord?"

"Why don't we just nuke the place," said Rachete.

Young Willem Brook was just putting a comb through his

shining hair, checking himself in the window while he was at it, stopped in the middle of his movement, somewhere on the top of his skull. "You are such an old fashioned man," he said. "Did you just say 'nuke'? That word has been out of fashion since Ronald Reagan was president."

"Who's Ronald Reagan?" said Rachete, gulping a mouthful of the black liquid back in his mug. "That coffee's so cold it's almost frozen into cubicles. Oh hell, I've had too much of it anyway. Listen, I'm getting tired of it. If those bacteria are so dangerous, what are we waiting for?"

"We don't want to attract any attention unless we have no other choice," said Brook. "Especially not in that location. It's an old wound from the Cold War and if word gets out we are still spooking around over there, there's going to be a lot of commotion up the chain of command. And you know what you always say, E.M."

"Yeah yeah," muttered Rachete. He hadn't taken his eyes off his monitor all this time, staring at the satellite images of the dark building in the snow.

"When the music stops up the chain of command, someone's going to sit down his fat ass on top of us down here," said Brook.

"I must stop saying that," said Rachete. "Anyway, it sounds worse coming from your mouth."

"What if we wait a little longer and then, if no one acts, we either march in or we drop some small bombs on it," said Brook.

"I'm very uncomfortable with the amount of parties

involved already. There's Chapman working for the competition. There's the Eco Warriors. There's four governments watching from a distance, including us, and all of them, I'm sure, ready to move in."

"You're forgetting the most dangerous party involved."

"I am?"

"The virus."

"Ah," said Rachete, looking really angry, "and that's why you are now picking up the phone and checking the army's status once again. Make sure they are on red alert, ready to move in if the situation changes. Let that Chapman do his work first. If he steals a sample, we take it from him and that'll save us a lot of time. Then we decide."

Brook picked up a phone to have the same conversation with his army contact he'd been having during the past few days. And the same question would remain unanswered: when does the situation change? When Chapman escapes from the building? When the Eco Warriors run off? When something explodes? When a helicopter arrives and takes off again?

What are we waiting for, Brook thought.

But he wasn't going to ask Rachete again. He was going to leave Rachete to look out the window, brooding on the whole situation, his back to the computer screens full of enlarges satellite images of the concrete building in the snow.

"What about that woman Chapman was with?" barked Rachete in the middle of the phone call.

"Woman? Huh?"

"He went there with a tourist. Where's she at?"

How would I know that, old man.

Thirty-six

The arrow looked at Carreidas from the other side on the room. It still rested on the stretched bow, as it had been for the past ten minutes. The woman was relentless, never easing her grip on the bow.

He had pretty much filled the ten minutes with talking, trying to persuade her not to kill him.

He thinks I'm going to kill him, Hitomi thought.

"Yes, the Ebola medicine is one hundred percent ready," said Carreidas.

"Then why test it on humans?"

"They want additional proof."

"You are sick," whispered Hitomi.

"Don't judge me too soon, lady," said Carreidas. "Like I said: the medicine works. These people are perfectly safe. Some may actually develop Ebola, some may not, we don't know why. But they'll all have the vaccine and be fine."

He looked at Hitomi, hoping for some kind of approval.

"Listen, it takes at least two full days for the virus to take effect, for the first signs to show. Long before they deteriorate, we will give them the medicine. All we need to test is if it works, we don't need to see the full disease at work."

"Bullsh*t," said Hitomi. "After a while, you'll want to know if your precious medicine also works for people who are close to death. That's how it works with scientists: they go on till the very end, way beyond reason. You'll want to know if you can cure someone who has a fever, muscular pain, a sore throad, headaches, the vomiting, diarrhea, liver and kidney failure, rash, internal and external bleeding and..."

"ALRIGHT!" shouted Carreidas. "You clearly know everything there is to know about Ebola. Listen, your friends..."

"They're not my friends."

"Your friends have been injected a couple of hours ago, six at the most. There's nothing to worry about."

"And when it's all over, you send everybody on a dog sleigh back to the civilized world, right?"

Silence.

"Well?"

Carreidas sighed. "Please lower that bow, it makes me nervous."

"I'm nervous too, so answer the question."

"I give you my word that no one will die of Ebola. I mean: *no one will have to die* as far as I'm concerned. I have the medicine. Get it? I'm a scientist in the business of saving people, not killing them."

He had wanted to tell her about the origins of Ebola. He truly had. But the woman never asked about that so he kept his mouth shut.

"What's the agenda?" said Hitomi. "Who decides, where and when?"

"People in high places decide. There's nothing I can do about that anymore. The power they have is just... I must report back in within twenty-four hours. I give the green light and then the top brass decide. Hell, lady, I'm just the scientist on duty; I don't know what happens next."

"But I do."

"Are you with those activists? Are you one of those people who believe that blowing things up is going to make the world a better place?"

But the Japanese woman had finished talking. She obviously didn't think the question was worth answering. She approached the scientist.

"Wait, lady, what are you...?"

Thirty-seven

Bruce woke up when a dim light was turned on in the corridor. Shortly after that, the glass door swooshed open. He immediately recognized Hitomi's slim silhouette as she stepped into his cubicle.

"Bruce, it's me," she whispered.

The dream was gone immediately and with it the memory of a sea of pain in which he had been slowly drowning. His upper arm hurt from the shot they had given him hours before and in the dream he had seen it turn green, with mushroom shaped things growing out of it, and dark liquids dripping down on his clothes, and screaming coming from all sides.

Now that the hurting arm turned out to be real, the screaming in the darkness must have been real as well.

"What happened?" he mumbled, trying to get a grip on his voice as his consciousness made an emergency landing in his head.

"Don't talk," whispered Hitomi. "Just follow me quickly."

"Wait Hitomi, I need that medicine first. They gave me a shot of the virus."

"I know. We are going to the lab. Just be quiet. And take this."

Hitomi gave Bruce his backpack. While he checked its contents quickly, they walked into the corridor.

Bruce saw that all the glass doors were open.

Carreidas appeared from one of the cubicles, supporting Forsythe, the leading man of the Eco Warriors, who looked pale and swaggered on his feet.

"If I had any strength left, I'd strangle you," said Forsythe.

Even if it was too soon for the Ebola virus to do its dirty work, the man was clearly not feeling well.

"You'll have your strength back when I get you the vaccine," said Carreidas. "Then you can do as you please."

"What's with him," whispered Bruce to Hitomi. "Is he suicidal?"

But Hitomi had already entered one of the other metal cubicles to assist Horatio, the second Eco Warrior. Horatio came out, being held up by Hitomi, looking even worse than his leader.

"We have to hurry," said Hitomi.

"We will," said Carreidas, as he appeared from another cubicle, supporting Rachelle, the third Eco Warrior.

Rachelle looked less fragile than her mail co-warriors, and more dangerous.

"Give me one reason not to kill you right now," she said with a hoarse voice, addressing Carreidas.

"Don't be stupid," said Hitomi. "We are not in the lab yet. You are going to be dead real soon if we don't get you the vaccine. The state you're in is not going to help if we run into the guards. Focus on getting there. It's two floors up."

The woman lifted one hand and patted the scientist on his cheek. "Good for you, doc. We're partners for a while longer. But don't get your hopes up."

Carreidas opened the door at the end of the corridor with a badge and the whole party moved into the hall beyond it. There were two ways out: an elevator and a stairway.

The elevator stood open, waiting for them.

They moved into it, some on their own, some supported by others. As a group, they looked pretty desperate.

"Hey big boy," said the Rachelle to Bruce. "Isn't it kind of curious that we are all as sick as hell, while you are perfectly alright?"

"It is indeed," said Bruce. "It must be in my genes."

After Carreidas had pushed a button and the elevator doors closed, he said: "It probably is. But it is still a chance of one in a million to be immune to Ebola."

"So that's what good genes look like," said Rachelle, smiling at Bruce and looking him up and down.

The elevator moved so fast that one of the Eco Warrior men threw up as a result of it.

Fortunately they were on the second floor almost immediately.

They entered another hall that led to a laboratory big enough to fill almost the entire second floor of the building.

In front of them, as well as to their left and right, were larges windows looking into a vast white space full of shelves and tables and spaces behind more glass.

Carreidas moved to a large door, opened it with his badge and pushed it open. "Come on! Quickly."

"What about the guards," hissed Bruce to Hitomi.

"They're having their rounds every hour and will be back within forty minutes," she replied. "But we may trigger some kind of alert by moving from one area to another, who knows."

"He'll know," said Bruce, pointing to Carreidas, who was leading the troupe towards a metal refrigerator.

"He assured me," whispered Hitomi, keeping her teeth together, "that they are not tracking his movements through the building or the use of his badge. Now do concentrate. Because after everybody gets his vaccine, you and I have to make sure no one gets the upper hand. We take the vaccine and get out. Got that?"

"Yes ma'am."

"Don't you yes ma'am me."

They got to Carreidas, who had opened the refrigerator and had taken out a large box full of vials, marked with handwritten labels that read "vaccine 08". Dozens. He attached one of the vials to a hypodermic syringe as fast as he could.

"Hurry doc," moaned Forsythe, "or you'll be vaccinating a corpse."

"Don't worry, this won't take long."

"One moment," said Hitomi, who had once again taken out her bow to make a gesture. "He gets it first." She pointed at Bruce.

There was some rolling of eyes and someone vomited again, but no one said anything.

"Now me," said Hitomi.

"You don't have Ebola," said Carreidas.

"This whole place is full of it," Hitomi said, through her teeth again. "Do it."

With her eyes, she brought Bruce's attention to the refrigerator and his bag. He seemed to be getting the point.

While Carreidas, after injecting Hitomi with the vaccine, got busy with the Eco warriors, Bruce grabbed another box from the fridge, the one that had "virus" written on every vial in it.

No one noticed. They were all focused on getting the injection.

Bruce let the box slide into the bag, trying to be as casual about it as he could. His brain worked overtime, trying to come up with a plan.

Hitomi's bow is not going to save the day, he thought. *We are going to need the works.*

"You will not feel a difference right away," said Carreidas, "because the virus has not taken its full effect yet and it will be killed before it can, if I may say so, blossom."

Carreidas put down the syringe after the last injection.

While they all stood there, rubbing their arms, feeling uncomfortable, Bruce let the other box of vials, the medicine, slide into his bag as well. He looked at Hitomi with a question mark on his face.

But before they could signal each other about the next step, Forsythe put an arm around Carreidas' neck, grabbed a surgical knife from the table with his other hand and put it to the scientist's throat.

Simultaneously, the other two members of the Eco Warriors grabbed items from the laboratory tables. Rachelle was suddenly in possession of a pair of scissors, which she held right before Bruce's face. Horatio came up with a large metal tray, which he held towards Hitomi like a shield against her arrows.

"Well," said Forsythe, "now that *you* have cured us all from this vile disease, we are going to go back to *our* original plan."

Hitomi and Bruce exchanged a brief look, trying to establish a modus operandi. But they hadn't prepared themselves for this, really.

"I agree," said Hitomi, nodding towards Bruce. "He's just going to sell this stuff to the competition."

"What!" yelled Bruce. Then he said to Forsythe: "Miss Sakamoto's the one who's trying to sell out, she's the one who's betrayed me ánd you!"

"Yeah," said Rachelle, "he's got a point there." She started to lower the scissors. "He's been exposed to the virus just like us, and we were captured when she was gone through the shaft, remember?"

"Don't believe any of those fairy tales," said Horatio, still holding the tray to protect himself from Hitomi's arrow.

"I don't believe in fairy tales myself," said Bruce, facing the scissors that came back up, closer to his face.

"Oh I believe in fairy tales," said Forsythe. "I just don't believe we can all live happily ever after."

Everybody froze.

He pressed the surgical knife harder against Carreidas' throat. "Only some of us live ever after, happy or not. Now... give me a *very* convincing reason why any of you should live beyond the tale. A reason that keeps us from killing you right here and right now. Remember: you tried to kill us first, herr doctor professor Carreidas!"

"I can give you that reason," said Bruce.

They all looked at him, including Hitomi.

"I have my hand in my bag, that is full of explosives," said Bruce. "That puts me in charge, so you better put down those surgical knives."

Bruce was not the only one thinking the word "BLUFF!" in capital letters. They were all thinking that right there and then. But that's the funny thing about bluff: are you ready to back it up or are going to back off? Even in the most blatant case of bluff — like Bruce's — it could still go wrong.

But before any of this could result in a standstill, a loud siren started to wail above their heads.

Thirty-eight

The glass entrance door opened up to four guards in black combat outfits wearing helmets and automatic rifles. Red lights started flashing from every direction, stroboscopic lights that blinded and confused.

"Don't move," one of the guards yelled.

Behind his back, Bruce had been frantically roaming around in his bag. While the men came running towards them, he took out his hand with force and released three objects into the air.

One of the men fired his rifle into the flying objects, but that didn't help. All three objects made a loud bang and started hissing, and then gave off a powerful white plume of smoke as they flew through the lab in different directions.

While the smoke started to cloud everybody's vision very quickly, Bruce threw a gas mask at Hitomi and started to put one on himself.

Before anyone could respond, the whiteness of the cloud had engulfed them all and had started to sting their eyeballs and throats. One dove to the floor, another fell onto a table, a third buckled and started to throw up; it was a mess with one thing in common: no one knew what they were doing any longer.

Except for Hitomi and Bruce. They had inhaled only a fraction of the gas from Bruce's projectiles but were now safe inside their masks. Bruce, being closest to the table where Carreidas had been standing, grabbed the entire box of vaccines, put it in his backpack and grabbed Hitomi by the hand to lead her out of this place.

Behind them, people tried to get up. Someone fired an automatic weapon, spraying bullets through the white smoke.

Closer to the door, Bruce took out another package from his bag and put it on a large computer console that stood against a wall. It stuck to the equipment with a clang, a magnet kissing a metal surface. A blinking red light on top of the package faded in the fog as Bruce and Hitomi rushed towards the exit.

From above, water started to rain down from the automatic fire extinguisher system.

While they kicked open a door in the hall and started running down the stairs, two guards emerged from the white cloud behind them — only to be blown aside by a large explosion that ripped through the computer console.

"Isn't it time you told me who you're working for, really?" Hitomi hissed to Bruce, who was only a couple of steps ahead of her.

"What if I did, Sakamoto? If I tell you I work for the good

guys you won't believe me and if I tell you I'm one of the bad guys you won't help me. So who cares?"

"Bruce Hillsborough Chapman, I *am* helping you. I got you out. So don't smart mouth me. I can tell if you're lying. I knew all along. But now that I know what's going on in this building, and I mean *exactly*, I must know what you know. Now *say* it."

Bruce kicked open a door that led into the basement. The dark grayness of the concrete corridors, damp and unpleasant, stretched before them.

"I work for the competition," he sighed. "But that doesn't necessarily mean it's bad. I need to make a living."

Echoes of their own running footsteps faded out in the darkness.

Thirty-nine

Hitomi and Bruce exited the Facility through its basement without being discovered. To avoid making any noises, they moved very slowly. When they stepped out into the cold air, they could hear noises coming from the building that towered above them. There was shouting, followed by gunfire.

As they started to run through the crevice, away from the building in the afternoon shades, they heard the sound of approaching helicopters.

"Funny how the cavalry always shows up late," Bruce panted, stumbling over the rocks in the shade.

"There is no cavalry going to help us," said Hitomi. "If we get caught with this stuff, you are going to have a very hard time explaining how we got it."

"Wait a minute," said Bruce, halting Hitomi by grabbing her arm. "What do you mean *I* am going to have a hard time? What about you?"

Hitomi smiled. "I am just a tourist, remember. I know people in high places who can vouch for me. But you... there is not a single thing about you that invokes any trust in people."

She jerked her arm away, still smiling, and continued running.

"Don't you even believe that my name is actually Bruce?"

But Hitomi speeded up as they approached the underground river crossing.

"It seems we are lucky," she said.

The river was now buried under a small mountain of ice and snow.

"Remember how a part broke off when you were swinging across?" said Bruce. "Apparently a lot more ice came down after we left here."

It made their way back a lot shorter. They reached the end of the crevice, where the steep path would lead them up the slope towards the high place where their snowmobiles rested.

Bruce stopped for a moment and looked back. In the falling dusk, helicopter flashlights searched the immediate perimeter of the concrete structure. Then he turned and looked up at the silhouette of the small Japanese woman, rushing up the snowy slope. A shadow drew across his face, and as the sounds of the helicopters faded away behind him, he started to follow her upwards.

The darkness unfolded slowly on the white hills. Behind Hitomi and Bruce, the helicopters were moving across the ice fields.

"What are they doing anyway? Do they think fugitives hide

on a white plain?"

Hitomi didn't reply.

Then one of the helicopters turned and started to fly across the crevice, straight at them. It threw large bundles of light towards the ground, swaying left to right and back. It was only a matter of time until one of the super trouper lights would hit the two running figures on the hillside.

Bruce cursed.

"You worry too much," said Hitomi. "Don't you feel it's starting to snow?"

"It is?"

A super trouper light hit them and this time it stayed on them, following their movements like a hungry mosquito.

"You going to defend us with an arrow now, Sakamoto?" barked Bruce as he slipped and slid.

Hitomi and Bruce continued running as the falling snow started to reflect the super trouper light from the helicopter into a white blur.

"Don't stop!" shouted Bruce. "We can make it."

While the snowfall grew thicker, sound faded into the distance and the helicopter abandoned the pursuit. All of a sudden, Hitomi and Bruce were alone in the crevice.

But they didn't stop running up that hill.

Forty

Hitomi and Bruce had reached the top of the first hill and made it to the edge of the forest. They were glad to get at least some relief from the falling snow. It was no longer falling vertically, but stinging into their faces, blown horizontally by a fierce wind.

They started the snowmobile engines. As they took off into the forest, the snowstorm subsided once again and Hitomi and Bruce could hear the sound of helicopters and shooting in the distance.

It wasn't until deep in the forest, much higher into the hills, that they stopped to consider their options.

"I hear no more helicopters," said Bruce. "That could mean they have forgotten about us. Or they're tied up in something else. I'm not sure if we can simply slide out of the forest on the other end. We'll be vulnerable out in the open."

"If we stay in the forest, the cold will kill us. But it'll kill neither the virus nor the medicine," said Hitomi. "On the other hand, it will be pretty harmless in this frozen land, so I can live with that."

They were sitting on the edge of their snowmobiles, facing each other.

"Spoken like a true Samaritan," said Bruce. "Do you have any idea how much money that stuff is worth? That stuff you're carrying around?"

They looked at each other.

"You want to try and take it from me?" said Hitomi. The white cloud coming from her mouth waited in front of her face before dispersing.

Bruce looked away. "That was a joke. We have to take it away from here to the civilized world at the very least. Being frozen here won't solve a thing. Someone is bound to find us sooner or later."

"I'll empty all the vials in the snow," said Hitomi. "If I have to."

While she said that, Hitomi realized that it was probably the most unbelievable piece of bluff Bruce had ever heard. And indeed, she saw him smiling as a result.

For a while, Hitomi looked on as Bruce got off the saddle and inspected his mobile, kicking the skis to check their suspension. He looked out of place.

"We," said Hitomi, "are going to get out of here and if I catch you even looking at the bag with the vials, I will put an arrow through you and the nearest birch tree."

His face darkening, Bruce said: "I've always wanted to be a tree-hugger."

He couldn't distinguish Hitomi's smile when she said:

"Liar."

Late in the evening, before they reached the edge of the boreal forest and the open plains, they stopped their snowmobiles once again and put up the tent between the trees. Above them was the thick layer of snow on top of the trees. No one was going to spot them from above.

While they installed for the night, after a long silence, Hitomi finally spoke.

"I don't criticize your actions, Bruce. What if you took a break from your mission and gave me a chance to convince you to choose otherwise?"

He smiled, but not enough to show it. He took his gloves back on and crawled inside.

When Hitomi crawled in after him, he laid back in the tent on a sleeping bag and looked at her.

"All right, have it your way, Hitomi. I take a break from my mission for the night. Hell, I'm tired of chasing viruses on my own. If it's so bloody important, how come not a single secret service from any country in the world is out here chasing it too?"

"For all I know they are all attacking that building right now," whispered Hitomi as she crawled closer to him. "But I guess it's a good question. We have a truce then?"

But she kissed him before he could answer.

Any noise they made was overcome by the hissing wind outside. Temperatures inside rose, outside they dropped even further for the night.

Forty-one

The first one to wake up after the smoke from Bruce's grenades had vanished into thin air, was Forsythe, the Eco Warriors' leader. It was the itching of his mustache that woke him up, the toxic gases clinging to the hairs and poking up his nose.

He immediately rose to his feet and saw a clear picture of the whole situation: Chapman and that woman had taken off and left them here in the pits. Forsythe realized he had to act quickly: within moments, the security people would wake up too and they would be hard to bargain with.

Immediately, Forsythe took charge of the situation. While kicking Rachelle, who was lying on the floor in an unflattening pose, he jerked an electricity chord from a table and began tying up all three security men. He also took their assault rifles from them.

"What the...," moaned Rachelle, "...what happened?"

"What hasn't?" barked Forsythe. "Nothing according to plan, that's for sure. Wake up Horatio, quickly. I figure all hell is going to break loose here very soon. We have to get out nów."

As it turned out, Horatio was already waking up.

So instead, Rachelle opened the cooling installation. "Vials are gone," she shouted, through the noise of the alarm, which was still sounding. "Chapman and that woman have them."

"Boy, were we sleeping," said Horatio. "When exactly did they take it?"

"While you were snoring," said Forsythe. "But hey, you can make up for all that by flying the chopper."

"What chopper?"

"The one that's standing in the courtyard."

When they came out of the elevator on ground level, the three Eco Warriors encountered more security personnel. But there were only two more of them, and they were no match for Forsythe's fury — especially not since he pumped all that fury out of his system through the assault rifle.

"That'll be enough killing, Forsythe," said Rachelle. "Man, you are blood-thirsty."

"I remember what these people tried to do to us. You should, too."

"They can't have gone far," said Horatio. "I don't have it down to the minute, but we were out for an hour at most."

"That's far enough," said Rachelle. "It's night. You plan to fly across the ice fields with your pocket light and look for them?"

They stood in the white light that lit the courtyard and

thought about this remark for a while.

"Either way, it doesn't matter," said Forsythe. "They will be sending people here very soon. There's an alarm system whaling — it's not going to go unnoticed. So looking for Chapman and the woman is the second thing to worry about. Let's move people. There's nothing for us here anymore."

They rushed to the helicopter in the middle of the courtyard. Forsythe touched his mustache with his hand and rubbed it in an attempt to stop the stinging. Horatio thought to himself something like: *Who's the real pilot of this machine? I haven't seen a pilot. Perhaps it was just one of the guards with a license to fly.* Rachelle brushed off her clothes with her hand, a white powder that had remained there after the grenade attack.

They got in.

Forty-two

You must decide.

Bruce stared at the roof of the tent, his eyes wide open, seeing nothing. But in his mind's eye he saw Hitomi, smiling at him. He saw nothing else.

You have been taken over by a woman.

Only now, in the silence of the arctic night, did Bruce realize he had brought Hitomi along not simply because he needed an alibi. He had also brought her along because she was the first woman in his life who impressed him with her strength and was not going to be ruled by him.

And that confused him profoundly. His actions had been influenced. Had things been the way they were, he would have killed her immediately upon escaping the Facility and taken the vials and escape. Now he was here, she was still here with him and right now she was not even pointing one of her lethal arrows at him.

Somehow she knows I will not harm her, he thought, much to his disgust. *She knows I could have left here there.*

In that same darkness, he saw his mother, her dress torn, her hair wild, hidden half behind his father who raised his fist again and again. And right before the memory played out and got to the point where his younger self raised a deadly kitchen tool, it ended. The whole dreamy vision ended because Bruce shook his head.

You once did something good, he thought.

His thoughts returned to Hitomi and her strength and her warmth…

Once, you did something good.

It was too painful.

He slid out of his sleeping bag, fully dressed, and put on his shoes in the absolute darkness — all this while he thought frantically. It was time to make up his mind. Beside him, Hitomi breathed quietly in the night.

His dead father danced before Bruce's eyes. After being hidden in the shadows of his mind for decades, his father had returned almost as powerful as he had once been in real life. And through it shone other images. It was as if all the events from long ago were bursting through an opening. Like a circus ensemble poured through the entrance of the main tent onto the arena, each member performing his act at the same time. All the wild horses and lions and acrobats; only the clowns were missing. There was no relief in the assembled acts — only fear, sweat and tears.

Nor was there and end in sight to the events unfolding; the arrest, the trial, the long years in prison, and with it the violence, the corruption, the abuse, when he found the primitiveness of his father to be replaced only by the primitiveness of a whole band of brothers.

And yet, in the middle of all this darkness and pain from long ago, he also remembered the justification that had lingered in his heart for a little while. For a few days, perhaps a few weeks after *it* had happened, he had simply known that he had done a good thing — even if the whole world around him treated him like a hard-core criminal. Young Bruce had done a good thing because his mother was a good woman who had stood up for him. For a moment he had thought no one was going to convince him otherwise.

But he had forgotten about that during the trial and his years in prison, until now, until Hitomi Sakamoto, that iron Japanese woman, had stood up for him and freed him from certain death in a metal cell with a glass door.

There was no denying it.

And it also changed nothing.

So was his life: there were these moments of clarity, of floating high above practicalities. And then back to reality.

By the time Bruce got to the snowmobiles, he had decided.

You must complete your mission, he thought. *Your reputation is on the line. Your money is already in the bank; you must now deliver the goods.*

He would take both virus and vaccine to safety of his employers.

While he disabled one snow mobile and mounted the other, he failed to rethink his position on Hitomi though. He thought confused thoughts about keeping her out of it, keeping her away from the spotlights in case he got caught.

In doing so, Bruce ignored his own impromptu decision to leave Hitomi in the middle of the forest without transport. As he mounted the snowmobile with the bag full of vials, and kick started the machine, the flood of thoughts was already leaving him.

He had lived a life of action, preferring to move forward any situation in an attempt to break through rather than wait for something to happen. That had made him a man who took a calculated risk, knowing that the average outcome of action was always better than the average outcome of waiting.

But as we all know, when the music stops, there's one chair missing on average.

In her half sleep, Hitomi sat on the back of a motorcycle, holding on to a boy in a leather suit as he sat bending forward, gassing up the engine. It roared and pulled her forward. She had her arms around his waist, and her face pressed against his drivers' suit, the cold surface stinging into her cheek.

Then she woke up from her dream with the speed of an arrow, shot from her bow.

She heard an engine roar close by, moving away quickly, and she unzipped her sleeping bag as fast as she could. With the other hand she touched the blackness of the night around her, feeling for her bow and arrows.

Forty-three

Outside the tent, the night had fallen silent. The wind had gone away, taking with it the snow filled clouds and its own howling. The forest held a canopy of snow, almost blocking the sky and its bright stars entirely. With it, an intense cold had taken over.

Hitomi immediately realized that she only had seconds to act. Without gloves, her hands would lose their grip quickly. Also, the object of her alarm moved away very fast: she saw only the dark shade of a man as he sped away on one of the snowmobiles. He also towed the second snowmobile, which accountant for his slow departure.

"Bruce Chapman," Hitomi yelled, reluctantly deciding to omit his middle name in a time of crisis, "stop right now."

The mobile sped on.

"Last chance!"

While this last chance instant fleeted by, Hitomi saw flashes of consequences, the results of the virus and its vaccine being in the wrong hands, the complications, the

feuding nations, the victory of greed over common sense —
and it was clear to her that Bruce Hillsborough Chapman was
the one who decided. Not her.

And she shot her arrow at the receding shadow.

Forty-four

Port Zodiac is as remote as harbors get. Positioned at the rim of a vast plateau and courting an arctic sea, it is uninhabited for ten months a year when the landscape is frozen solid in all directions.

The perfect hideout for a woman with the world's most wanted virus in her possession, Hitomi thought.

She had decided not to return to the villa, where she and Bruce had started their adventure. Even though there was all the equipment she needed, such as fuel and communications equipment, she had felt it would be the first place anyone would come looking for her.

Instead, she had stayed inside the forest as long as she could, unseen for the helicopters that passed overhead a couple of times. She had sped through it on her snowmobile. After about fifty kilometers she'd had to leave the forest and take her chances out in the open. Hitomi had made many outdoor journeys before and she knew how to read a map. There was no doubt in her mind that she would reach Port

Zodiac before nightfall. From the edge of the forest it was only another hour on the snow mobile.

And she had been right. The dark silhouettes of buildings and containers, partially covered by snow, beckoned her from the distance in the twilight. There was even an abandoned cargo ship, its hull hovering over every other structure, lying perfectly still in the frozen sea.

There was not a single column of smoke from a chimney.

The first place to go to would be the communications center. There was a large white sphere on top of a small building. It was basically a shed, albeit entirely made of concrete. Inside, Hitomi knew, would be the internet connections and access to telephone lines. But it was the sphere on top of the roof she was going for. It contained a homing beacon for ships on the dark, icy seas. Even though Port Zodiac was completely fenced in by ice this time of year, large parts of the waters were accessible for ships. They all needed the Port Zodiac homing beacon.

As soon as it was turned off, someone would notice and send a crew over to repair it. That was not going to take very long, she guessed.

That crew would be Hitomi's way out.

Providing no one from the Facility tracks me down here first, she thought.

Hitomi parked the snowmobile next to the concrete shack and walked around until she found the ladder leading up to the roof. The whole building had only one level, so it was a very short climb. The steel ladder was covered with a layer of ice and Hitomi almost slipped. The roof presented her with an ice rink, almost impossible to walk on. She decided to crawl to the middle of the shed, where the white sphere was mounted on a small tower of steel.

As soon as she got to the center and saw the cables, Hitomi realized that there was no way she was going to cut one of them or unscrew a hatch that led to the power supply. The cables were encased in white steel tubes and all the screws were frozen. On top of that: she didn't have any equipment. So she decided to go down and try to force her way into the shed, using a pocketknife or something of the sort.

Half an hour later, Hitomi stood inside the small building and pulled down the lever of the power supply.

We're up and running. Now find a warm place to hide until a crew shows up.

She drove the snow mobile through the tiny harbor towards a large warehouse. After parking the mobile behind some crates she tried the personnel entrance.

It wasn't locked.

They must think there's not a burglar on the entire continent.

Inside the warehouse she saw a large crane-and-rail system developed for the stacking and distributing of small crates. It was full of robot arms and rails and overhead rails and walkways. In the back was a series of small offices and toilets.

Hitomi walked around, tried every door until she found a

small office with a window that looked out on the shed with the sphere.

Here I can see them coming, she thought.

Even though she felt she had prepared herself for everything, the humming sound in the distance startled her. It closed in rapidly.

A helicopter.

Because the window looked towards the sea, Hitomi ran out of the office towards the large entrance doors and peeked out the personnel door.

A black steel bird hovered across the white plain, straight at her.

They must be guessing, thought Hitomi.

Her snow mobile could not have left a clear trace in the hard, frozen snow. And even if it did, whoever was flying that aircraft would not be able to see the trace from that altitude.

Doesn't matter now. This is not my rescue party.

Hitomi closed the door quickly. It was too late to worry about the snow mobile. She hoped it would remain unseen behind the crates.

Quickly she ran through the building, looking for a place to hide. It was going to be impossible to escape from this place unseen, she now realized. The terrain was white in all directions.

You can spot an ant without a magnifying glass at a hundred meters.

She would have to wait till nightfall. But even then... where could she go?

Relax, lady. Find out who's in the helicopter first.

Forty-five

By the end of the afternoon only the wind remained.

The helicopter's engine had been roaring for quite some time, hovering over Port Zodiac, going back and forth, checking out this location and that, and finally faded.

Typically for the Northern landscape, the sun went down early. The night cold took over quickly, forcing temperatures to drop rapidly from around the freezing point downwards.

For a while, Hitomi thought the helicopter had probably vanished entirely, moving back to where it came from. But this shimmer of relief vanished with a shock when she heard the main warehouse door open.

People were coming in. Whoever they were, they deserved credit for trying to enter as quietly as possible. However, they failed miserably. There were clattering noises of metal boxes shattering across the floor. Someone cursed. There was a short burst of whispered arguments.

"We know you are here," a voice yelled.

Rachelle, Hitomi thought. *They saw my snowmobile.*

"Give us the virus and the vaccine, Chapman. Then we can go our separate ways. We will deliver it into safe hands, away from commercial corporations. We will also make sure you get paid whatever fee you were supposed to get. Just as long as you get one thing right: we are determined to get it from you. There is too much at stake to let you have the Ebola vaccine and take it to yet another bunch of greedy capitalists."

The three Eco Warriors split up and started to walk in different directions.

Bundles from flashlights beamed through the industrial space of the warehouse. There were noises and there were voices talking back and forth.

It seemed to Hitomi they didn't care about their safety that much. They were easy target for anyone with a gun — or with a bow for that matter. But it would probably be best to wait and do nothing for a while. They were probably not going to find her; at least not in the way they were rambling about.

"Light, anyone?" someone yelled. It was the thin Horatio, obviously, cunning as always.

There was a loud *bang* and luminescent tubes started to light the place. They popped on one by one, a long row of bright white lights, some of them flickering only, some of the covered in dust and cobwebs, and some of them blocked by high stacks of crates or a large crane. Together they lit up the place pretty well.

The threesome started to comb the place with increasing restlessness.

From high up, Hitomi looked at the Eco Warriors as they

roamed the place, kicking open office doors, rummaging through all the toilets and urinals, walking around the stacks of crates, and opening the doors to crane cabins.

Forsythe climbed into one of the crane cabins and switched on the controls. The electrically operated machine suddenly started to move and the cabin went upwards. The machine looked like an octopus, with many long feet and grabbers pointing towards the ground and its steering hut on top. It rose and rose and reached the level of the ceiling walkways. There, it halted.

"Guys, there's a whole labyrinth of walkways up here," yelled Forsyth.

"Well, go check it out," Rachelle echoed back. "Hurry up. Before they catch up with us."

By that time, Hitomi had already withdrawn to the darkest corner of the ceiling walkway. She watched Forsythe as he moved in on her.

Forsythe was getting really irritated.

As far as he was concerned, they could have been out of this ice world a long time ago if that Chapman dude hadn't take the virus and the vaccine and run off. Now they were chasing him across the Arctic and they were basically hurrying nowhere.

They had simply looked at the map and gambled. Where does one go from the Facility, when one doesn't want to be seen or found, but still be able to make a run for it? The villa had been location number one. But it had been empty. There were two other destinations that made sense. One was a freighter railway. The other one was Port Zodiac.

First they had flown to the railway, but after hovering above the tracks for a while they realized there was nothing to gain. There was no train in sight. If Chapman had gotten on board of a train, he would have to jump on it and leave his snowmobile behind.

Anyway, they saw nothing as far as the eye could see, so Zodiac Harbor had automatically become the logical next stop.

But perhaps they had underestimated that Chapman.

Here we are, still in the doldrums, still without the virus and the vaccine, and there's still a risk of coming home empty handed, he thought.

Then he suddenly felt something sting in his neck. A knife? A syringe? It came from the shadows and then moved away again.

Baffled, Forsythe halted and turned his head right, albeit extremely slow. At his right was another walkway. On it stood Hitomi Sakamoto. She pointed her Japanese bow at him.

"What the hell...," said Forsythe. He felt his neck where he had been stung; he was sure of that now.

"Be very quiet," hissed Hitomi, widening her eyes, giving him her fiercest look, even if he was probably unable to see it in the half-light under the building's ceiling.

"What's that you said?" someone yelled from below.

"Nothing," replied Forsythe. And then whispered to Hitomi: "What do you want? What'd you sting me for?"

"I injected you," whispered Hitomi. "You now have Ebola again."

"Stupid woman. I already had Ebola and I've already had the vaccine. So what'd you do that for? And where's Chapman? Are you an agent? What are you?"

"It doesn't matter," whispered Hitomi. "I've decided we must work together. You get the vaccine and I get the virus."

"No way."

"Fine. Then die." Hitomi made a gesture as if she was going to walk away. "You know, you can't be sure that vaccination will protect you a second time?"

Forsythe hissed through his teeth. "Where do you have the vaccine?"

"It's not on me, if that's what you mean. I hid it."

"Clever woman. You should join us."

The conversation started to relax Forsyth a bit. "What will you do with the virus once we're out of here?"

"None of your business. You just get the vaccine to the authorities. That's what you wanted, isn't it? Get the vaccine out of the hands of the greedy pharmaceutical industry? Well, you can have it if you give up your chase. We really should be working together to avoid getting caught by whoever raided that Facility."

Forsythe shrugged. "Some government bureau. They would love to get their hands on the vaccine, I can tell you that. They are stuck in the Facility because we disabled their transport, but it is probably not going to take them a long time to fix it or get help. Listen, I'll talk to the others."

"You do that."

"Where's Chapman?"

"What do you care? I have the stuff, that's what matters."

Forsythe gave her a long look. "It's a long flight out of here. Are you going to point that bow at me all the way?"

"Do I have to?"

Forsythe sighed. He was getting tired of arguing. "I suppose not. You have a point."

"Good," said Hitomi. "Get your pals and I'll tell you my plan. We are taking the helicopter you've use to get here and I'm sitting in the back."

Forty-six

Soon, the bouquet of flowers would lose all its colors and hide underneath a layer of the brightest white ripe. Hitomi looked at it and felt sad.

Is that a wolf? she thought.

Hitomi stared at the flowers and the stone and listened to the howling in the distance; or at least that's what she thought it was. On the other hand, it could also be the wind, playing its melodies on the instruments of the earth, the trees and the rocks.

The mountainous landscape, the forests, the snow and the ice, it was a good home for wolves, she thought.

Whether it would also be a good home for Bruce Hillsborough Chapman, remained to be seen.

The sand around the newly dug grave was yet unfrozen. But everything was ready for the retreat into winter. The coffin down there. And the stone, with Bruce's full name on it.

Except for the flowers. They would have a short life.

The snow creaked behind her. Hitomi didn't look up until a

man reached the grave and stood next to her.

They exchanged a short glance.

"Miss Sakamoto?"

"Yes."

"My name is E.M. Rachete. I have some information about Mr. Chapman if you want it."

Hitomi looked at the horizon. "You picked a strange moment to share that with me, Mr. Rachete. What does your E.M. stand for anyway?"

"Ellis Markham." Then he laughed. "Never in my life has anyone ever asked that. Why do you want to know?"

"Because you are disturbing me and I want to address you properly," Hitomi snarled. "Now listen, Ellis Markham Rachete, tell me whatever it is you want to get rid of and then leave me alone."

"I work for a government agency that has been looking into Mr. Chapman's affairs for a long time," said Rachete. "We're called the Bureau. We were monitoring him and he led us to the location of the Facility where Everest has been working on the virus and the vaccine. We moved in with half an army shortly after he went there, hoping to get our hands on the merchandise."

"Are you in the habit of making your move a little late, Ellis Markham?"

Again, Rachete laughed.

"Could you stop laughing," Hitomi said. "I am standing here to mourn a friend. I find it inappropriate."

She didn't sound unfriendly at all, though.

"And why are you being so vague?" asked Hitomi. "Why do you say 'a government' when you and I both know perfectly well what country you're working for? Why do you say 'virus' when you know it is called Ebola?"

"You are right. I apologize," said Rachete. "We flew across borders. Pretty dangerous, politically speaking, so you can forgive my vagueness, yes? I do not want to say anything that can create problems for you in the future. You know more than I do. I don't need to say anything that can be recorded with a hidden microphone and used against me or the Bureau. Now, do you want to know about Chapman, yes or no?"

Hitomi shrugged. "Sure."

Is that a wolf? she thought, but it was hard to tell with this man, standing next to her, talking all the time.

"He is a loner," said Rachete.

"*Was*," said Hitomi.

Rachete started again. "Chapman was a loner. A gun for hire, you might say. We do not know his true identity. Chapman is probably not his real name for we have been unable to put his life's history together. He just shows up in our files some twenty years ago as being connected to several cases, most of them unsolved. He worked for whoever paid the most. As an assassin, we presume, but also just as an investigator. There have been many cases of industrial espionage around the world: businesses or nations stealing each other's secrets. Stuff that is kept from the media, like a fire that burns underground while the world thinks everything's fine. Only the specialists know there's a fire. If

George Bush had sent Chapman to Iraq, there would have been no debate about whether Saddam Hussein's regime produced weapons of mass destruction. You get my drift?"

"I'm not sure if I get it, but I can sure smell it."

That response confused Rachete for a moment. He had done a lot of smoking the other night. And drinking. And his coat was...

He shrugged off these thoughts.

"Chapman was hired by large corporations, or sometimes governments, to steal back secrets, or find out stuff in general. If you wanted to find some secret facility, he was one of the best noses for hire."

"No need to call a man a nose," said Hitomi.

"We have been on his trail for three years because he seemed to be involved in something big. An antidote to Ebola, that Everest wanted to keep to themselves. Our lab guys also had the idea that Ebola might have been... well... a deliberate act."

"So?"

"The proof of all that would be in the Facility. Only... we couldn't find it. Been searching for years. Kept several Everest employees under surveillance. But there was simply no connection to be found. When we discovered that Chapman was looking into Everest as well, we decided to change our strategy and focus on him."

Hitomi nodded.

It's getting cold.

In the distance, the sun was nearing the mountaintops.

"Unfortunately, there is nothing left in the Facility. Samples, computer files... That huge fire destroyed everything of value on the laboratory floor. There is only one option."

"And that is?"

"You took it."

Hitomi shrugged. "Me? Look here, Rachete, I am just a tourist. Chapman was my guide in the wilderness, I hired him through the hotel and he took me to a house out there for some skiing and sleighing and bow shooting. That's all."

"Sure you did. But I also think you were inside the Facility with Mr. Chapman. That whole wild trip was just his cover. It was you who told the local authorities where to find his body. I heard the recording of your phone call. It was your voice. You shot him with your bow, Miss Sakamoto. They don't know you are an expert on the Japanese bow, but I do. I think you shot him when the two of you ran off with the virus and the vaccine. We interrogated the scientists out there. I know."

"I'm tired," said Hitomi. "Can you get to the point?"

"And I'm cold," said Rachete. "I'll get to it now. Listen, I don't care about any of this. But if there is a virus, it had better be destroyed in the fire. And if there is a vaccine, it should get into the hands of the right people. I've looked into your background. I know who you are and who you work for. Miss Sakamoto, you are the producer of the world's number one business talk radio show. You have friends in high places. I have made inquiries and I am told that you are to be trusted. Your boss is going to raise hell if I put you on the stand. Anyway, I trust you. Just tell me: is it safe?"

Rachete stood there in the cold, smelling of nicotine and garlic and alcohol, feeling bad about that now that he was eyed by this handsome Japanese woman of his own age — for quite a long time.

Should I tell her I normally don't smell like this?

"Is it safe?"

"I took it from Chapman when it became clear he was going to sell it to the highest bidder. Then I put everything in a pot, I boiled it and mixed it with bleach. Are you satisfied now?"

"Not really. How'd you get bleach in the middle of nowhere?"

"You'd be surprised."

Hitomi stared into Rachete's eye without moving a muscle in her face.

Then she said, with emphasis: "I went back to the civilized world. No big deal. On the snowmobile. Go back to your... *nineteen-eighty-four office* and start the next job. Mission accomplished."

"No need to be sarcastic, Miss Sakamoto," said Rachete. "Your snowmobile was found in Port Zodiac." He raised his hand to silence a possible response from her. "No need no comment. If you are feeling safe, them so am I. Goodbye Miss Sakamoto."

He nodded and walked away, creaking in the snow.

Hitomi sighed. The sun was finally setting on Bruce Hillsborough Chapman's last resting place.

Too bad, Bruce. You were in good shape.

Forty-seven

The terrace lay in the sun, which shone between the buildings on the other side of the street. It would only be there for a short time, the sun, before it would move on behind one of the towers of glass and concrete. But the small group of people at the table next to the potted bushes behaved as if the sunshine would last a lifetime.

They were celebrating. Spilled champagne was on the table. There were only the three of them on the entire terrace as it was still early in the morning, but they were making noise as if the place was completely crowded and all seats were taken.

"Here's to the Red Cross," said Forsythe. This morning he had already said that seventeen times. It was most unusual behavior for the leader of the Eco Warriors.

But the pressures of the past weeks were finally wearing off. Ahead was the confrontation with the higher echelons of the Eco Warriors; picky people who were going to question every detail of the operation, who were going to complain about taking 'unnecessary risks', 'jeopardizing the entire operation', 'acting without consulting head quarters' and 'giving away the century's most important vaccine to the Red Cross with complete and utter disregard of the Warriors' vested interests'.

With all of that coming, this was their last chance to let it all go.

"I propose a toast also to our mysterious aids Hitomi and Bruce,' said the woman, the only member of the little troupe who was not visibly intoxicated. "We still don't know who they are and who they work for, but they saved the day."

Horatio slid away into a sober mood. He pushed his champagne glass further away on the table. "I hope you still feel that way a few days from now," he said. "When we are back and you are facing the inquisition. They are not going to accept our story of two unknown people, who have taken the vaccine and then vanished."

"Hitomi saved us, didn't she?" said the Rachelle. "It doesn't matter who she really is."

Horatio hammered the table with his fist. This spooked the approaching waiter; he bent backwards and saw the bottle of champagne, along with a large bowl of nuts, slide to the ground.

While the waiter grabbed the bottle before it hit the floor, in a rain of bouncing nuts, Horatio barked: "They are going to call us unfit for the job. Some unknown *petite* with a Japanese bow took over and kicked our behinds into submission? She saved us from death by Ebola? That's what you're going to say? How is that going to earn you any points?"

Forsythe rose from his chair, bent over to Horatio and shouted: "YOU WORRY TOO MUCH." Then he burst with laughter.

The other two smiled along with him. Then, slowly, they joined in a fit of laughter.

"It's going to be degradation day!"

Their howling, their laughter... not a sound of it penetrated the glass of the building on the other side of the streets: the Palais Carinth. Four floors higher a young woman looked down at the small cars and the parasols hiding most of the terraces.

Suddenly she turned. Behind her, the executive meeting room door was opened and a man in a pin striped suit entered. He crossed the entire room, which was quite an endeavor because he had to walk all around the oval oak conference table with all of its twenty-seven chairs.

"Excuse me, Miss Rhondinova," he said, when he finally stood in front of her, "I must ask you to make up your mind about the reservation of the executive boardroom and suites." His voice was aristocratic and could be interpreted as demeaning, unless seen as a conference hotel manager's way of keeping a professional distance. No need to be friends with the guests here.

"They are paid for, right?"

"They are indeed," he said. And then, after hesitating for a moment under the scrutinizing look of the tall, slim woman in her dark suit, her black hair pointing straight down like a metal shield, and her pointy dark glasses, he continued: "Please note that there are no complaints whatsoever, Miss Rhondinova."

"Then I don't see the problem."

"Not a problem. I hope you don't mind me offering you my assistance in this way, Miss Rhondinova."

"Your assistance?"

"Yes. You have been here for a whole week now, either in your room or in the restaurant or in this boardroom. Your employers have not shown up. You seem unable to decide what course of action to follow, if I may be so bold."

"That is very kind of you," said the woman, clicking one of her very high heels on the parquet floor. "I must apologize for this... situation. My employers are the ones who pay for the boardroom and the suites, they ask me to plan things and so forth. They have..."

"Yes?"

"They have..."

"Please be advised that I will be very discreet with any information you give me, Miss Rhondinova. You have been a good client for many years. I am accustomed to our guests operating with the necessary secrecy. Movie stars. Media moguls. You have your reasons for wanting to avoid the limelight, I trust. Your secret is safe with me. Perhaps I can help you plot a course of action. I will be candid with you too: if the spaces you've rented are not being used, we have many other clients who would be eager to use them instead."

"I have been unable to reach my employers," the woman

said hastily. She threw out the words, confirming the hotel manager's assumption that she was at a loss of options.

"You've asked their office?"

"They don't have an office. All I have ever had, was a phone number far from here. That number remains... unanswered. And then again, they always called me anyway. Without instructions I am... in a cul-de-sac."

The hotel manager smiled.

I have use for a woman who uses the expression 'cul-de-sac', he thought.

"I think I can help you, Miss Rhondinova," he said, allowing a faint smile on his face.

She didn't respond. Looked down the street again.

"A woman like you, with your skills, is extremely valuable to this venue. I offer you a job in a leading position — or any position you have an appetite for. You can start right away, at hours of your choosing. There is enough restructuring and organizing to be done here. I'm sure you are very qualified, from what I've seen you do through years, being our guest regularly."

The woman turned and looked at the hotel manager, surprised.

He patted her on the arm. "If they have failed to give you word for a whole week, you must presume they are not going to give you any word ever again, miss Rhondinova. Think about it for a while and let me know."

He wanted to turn and walk away. But as he expected, the woman made up her mind immediately.

"I accept your offer," she said.

The angry thoughts about Lord Rand and Locarn she had been entertaining, faded away. They had always paid her in advance. The business had been good for many years, allowing her a lot of freedom in the intermediate months when there were no meetings. And perhaps the end had come too sudden — but it was just as well.

They were probably shot in some remote country, for being total assholes.

What if I know too much?

No, don't worry. No one knows I worked for them.

Rhondinova followed the hotel manager out of the boardroom. She didn't look back.

Forty-eight

A fresh load of snow had been dumped on the country by a raging force. But its powers were spent and now the sun reigned once again, turning the soft whiteness into a blinding fury.

Both Hitomi and her grandfather wore handmade sunshields: a thin stroke of thick paper tied to the ears, with a thin slit in the middle right in front of the eyes. They could see proper, without being blinded all the time.

"Ask yourself about justice before you shoot your arrow and kill," whispered grandfather Sakamoto.

He had folded the paper sunshield for her. It would be her first lesson in shooting in the blinding white landscape and learning to see just as sharp as the rabbit they were after.

The wind blew towards the rabbits in the snow. The animals were small, but they were close enough for Sakamoto's eleven years old pupil Hitomi, who was already a master at many combative arts. He had witnessed her karate teacher swallowing his own lessons.

"What justice?" asked Hitomi, hissing through her lips, a white plume of breath rising in the cold sunlight.

"If you kill without justification," whispered grandfather, "your prey's host will haunt you and bring misery upon you. Just as you will be wreaking havoc upon your own killer if it is done without the proper respect for *karma*."

"So I must ask why the rabbit must be killed?" whispered Hitomi.

"Precisely."

"Why must the rabbit be killed?"

"Because it is its flesh's purpose to serve as food and its skin's purpose to serve as clothing," said grandfather. "Also, if we do not use the rabbit in this way, there will soon be too many of them and all our crops will be destroyed. That will be as bad for the rabbits as it will be for man. So get on with it, girl."

Hitomi liked her grandfather's practical approach of spiritual things. Karma meant food on the table, as far as he was concerned.

"Every battle has an outcome," said grandfather, "and every outcome has a purpose. The trick lies in discovering what that purpose is."

The arrow whooshed from Hitomi's bow towards its purpose.

"The moment of decision is the culmination of all previous achievements. There is no turning back once the decisive movement has begun. This crossroads is a place of relief, of abandoning all control, of simply moving forward. Within that lies the possibility of regret, of error, and one must realize that the wrong decision is still a decision. It will still move you forward towards the next crossroads. Therefore it can never be really wrong; at most it can be a detour on your journey.

The arrow is shot.

But the winter landscape lies low, hiding under its burden."

—From the diary of Hitomi Sakamoto

THE

HITOMI

FILES

Acknowledgements

The writing of North has been an adventure. It took me through the eventful history of medicine and epidemics, and it took me to locations throughout the world. Except for the birthplace of Hitomi Sakamoto, being Japan, I've felt no need to reveal the names of these locations. Once upon a time, readers knew little of the world outside their own town or city or province, and it was up to the authors of the world to take them places. Those days are gone. The world is small and except for the bottom of the ocean, everything is familiar by now. I feel we should put our imagination back to work and one way of doing this is allowing you, the reader, to travel in your own mind.

Even if all I had to do was follow Hitomi in her stride, I would not have come this far if not for the support and dedication of several people. Natalie Wright was my premier beta reader, and a demanding one too, followed up by Hanno Koch and Dave Thomas. Roger Hale's enthusiasm for my Radio Detective series has spurred me always and has helped Hitomi Sakamoto rise to the occasion. Dane of ebooklaunch.com did a superior job on the cover design, capturing precisely what I wanted to express, and more, and designed the Hitomi logo. And above all this novel thanks its existence to my partner Harriet, who has always supported my writing through turbulent times, and who definitely has the Hitomi touch. Or is it the other way around?

M.H. Vesseur

Request from the author

Thank you for reading Hitomi Sakamoto's first adventure. I hope you enjoyed it and will be willing to write a review on the platform of your choice, like Amazon, Apple iBooks, Kobo or Goodreads. Making that extra effort is greatly appreciated by other readers... and of course by me. Thank you! I hope you and I stay connected through Twitter, Facebook, Google+, Pinterest or my free email newsletter. I'll make sure you'll stay tuned. Have a good evening/night/day!

M.H. Vesseur

Twitter @MHVesseur

Facebook www.facebook.com/MHVesseur

Subscribe to M.H. Vesseur's mailing list on www.mhvesseur.com

About the author

M.H. Vesseur has written many short stories for literary magazines in The Netherlands, Belgium, Canada and the U.S.A. He was awarded for the best debut with his first story. In his radio detective series about Carl Pappas he has now written and published the seven short crime novels *CEO Groupie*, *Die Rich*, *Tax Me If You Can*, *Acid Asset*, *Nosedive*, *Power Play* and *Blood Border*. The radio detective's producer Hitomi Sakamoto now stars in her own series, which begins with *North*. M.H. Vesseur also published the novel *Lemniscate*, a collection of literary short stories called *Allusions* and his outlook on the super economy *Burning Neil Armstrong*. M.H. Vesseur is an awarded advertising copywriter. He lives in the forests of The Netherlands.

www.mhvesseur.com

Other works by M.H. Vesseur

You can find a complete overview of M.H. Vesseur's works on www.mhvesseur.com. Most books are available as paperbacks and ebooks through Amazon, Apple iBooks and Kobo.

BURNING NEIL ARMSTRONG — The economy is evolving from a man made theory of labor and money towards an autonomous, endless event. Even the wildest conspiracy theory becomes obsolete in the light of this emergence, for no one controls it. And so the economy will continue to grow. M.H. Vesseur, author of speculative stories for literary magazines, expands this prediction and describes the definitive form of a super economy that will soon arrive and forever crush our memories of a better future that once beckoned us. Burning Neil Armstrong is unforgiving.

ALLUSIONS — A short story collection, containing several stories published previously by literary magazines. Contains *In Snuff Park*, *Babyface Junkie*, *Narcissist Guru*, *Sketches of a Worldwide Christo and Jeanne-Claude*, *Beloved Stalker* and *Territory Game*.

CEO GROUPIE (a Radio Detective) — One night three live guests join Carl Pappas on his radio show The Boardroom: two CEOs and a woman who calls herself: "the CEO Groupie". When the mysterious woman reveals the existence of a secret call girl organization for CEOs and subsequently disappears a couple of days later, the bizz jockey engages on a search. What happened to the CEO Groupie and what are the other two guests up to? Together with his radio team — his producer Hitomi Sakamoto and his sound engineer Don Wozniak — Carl Pappas sets out to deal with this.

DIE RICH (a Radio Detective) — Carl Pappas, the bizz jockey, goes on the air again. His radio show "The Boardroom" is both loved and feared by the global business community. He has a sharp eye for business news and the big mouth of a talk radio host. This time around he has some very wealthy guests joining him on his show: two billionaire entrepeneurs and their future successors, who also happen to be their sons. Of course it doesn't take the bizz jockey a very long time to upset some of his guests and his audience — and that same night the bizz jockey finds himself heading into dangerous waters, in the hands of some very angry rich people. His team — producer Hitomi Sakamoto and sound engineer Don Wozniak — is forced to go out and rescue their reckless boss. And then there are the rich kids they have to deal with...

Tax Me If You Can (a Radio Detective) — Carl Pappas, the bizz jockey, is cooking up a real shocker: during a live broadcast of his popular business talk radio show "The Boardroom" he plans to reveal secrets about tax dodging practices around the globe. In the middle of the preparations he and his producer Hitomi Sakamoto face unexpected trouble. Who is trying to shut the Bizz Jockey up in this quiet country under the tropical sun? Is it the local military junta? Is it the business community? Or is the sun finally getting to Carl Pappas' head?

ACID ASSET (a Radio Detective) — Carl Pappas, the bizz jockey, is feeling good about the prospects of environment-friendly plastics he's discussing on his radio show "The Boardroom". But as he soon finds out there's something not right with the company behind it. Can the bizz jockey protect a lonely scientist against the schemes of a large corporation that smells money? Or will he be unable to stop a revolutionary asset from becoming really acidic? Buckle up for a race against arsonists, corporate crime, dogs, bullets and a dangerous industrial zone in the middle of a blizzard, softened only by some real team spirit.

NOSEDIVE (a Radio Detective) — When a large corporation is struck by a cripling strike among its workers and an apparent terrorist attack on its factory, bizz jockey Carl Pappas steps forward to offer his public support.

But as he soon finds out, there's more to the picture than meets the eye. Why is the owner hiding in her large mansion?

What happened in her youth that is threatening her after all these years? It's a job for the radio detective — and this time around his boss gives an unexpected hand.

POWER PLAY (a Radio Detective) — The death of an environmental activist brings bizz jockey and unofficial "radio detective" Carl Pappas to the quiet island of Islasol. Everything seems to be OK with the local National Park and the wind turbine park in the heart of it.

But Carl and his team soon find out you can't take anything on face value. Below the surface of an environment friendly enterprise lies a darker secret. It's time for the radio detective to unravel the local secrets of wind energy, assisted by his producer Hitomi and a new, unlikely ally.

BLOOD BORDER (a Radio Detective) — The inhumanity of human trafficking is forcing the radio detective to make a stand. So in the midst of politics and public outrage, Carl Pappas and his team infiltrate the trafficking cartel of a man known as The Clown. But there is nothing funny about it, for the radio detective soon finds himself in the lion's den, a place crowded with former narcotics traffickers and their violent ways. Will they be able to do something about the screaming injustice of immigration or will they become prey themselves?

<<<<>>>>